This New Life

This New Life

Sheila Jacobs

© Copyright 2001 Sheila Jacobs
ISBN: 1-85792-661-7

Published by Christian Focus Publications Ltd,
Geanies House, Fearn, Tain, Ross-shire
IV20 1TW, Scotland, Great Britain
www.christianfocus.com
email: info@christianfocus.com

Cover illustration by Graham Kennedy, Allied Artists.
Cover design by Owen Daily

Printed and bound by Cox & Wyman, Reading.

O LORD, you have searched me and you know me…I praise you…your works are wonderful, I know that full well.
(Psalm 139 vv1,14)

MASSIVE THANKS TO:

Everyone who has prayed during
the writing of this book;
to Hannah Burton
for giving me an idea -
And of course, to my mum, Mary Jacobs,
for the encouragement, support, patience
and unending cups of tea.

*Go…tell the people the full
message of this new life.*
(Acts 5:20)

Contents

How it all began

There was a new girl in my class called Stacy Morgan and no-one liked her.

This was because she was always talking about how much she wanted to be an actress and bored anyone who'd listen with incredibly dreary tales about how she planned to go to Stage School one day. She also used big words like 'preposterous' a lot and irritated everyone. Including me.

Which is why I wasn't very happy when my mum said I ought to be friends with her.

"You're joking!" I said.

But she wasn't. Because in my mum's brain the very fact that Stacy, her mum and dad and baby brother had come to our church once or twice, meant I must instantly have loads in common with the silliest girl in the school.

My friend Amanda was quite disapproving.

"Why do you keep inviting that awful girl to hang around with us?" she asked.

Dolefully, I tried to explain that my mum felt I should make an effort to be nice to Stacy because her family had indicated an interest in God, so I should show Stacy by example that Jesus loved and accepted her. But Amanda wasn't a Christian and said if God wanted to show Stacy Morgan he loved her, couldn't he find a different way other than have her eat her lunch with us every day? I had to admit, she had a point.

9

I was feeling especially gloomy about Stacy one windy October evening. This was due to her unwanted presence, sitting on my bed, swinging her legs so that her heels clicked in an annoying rhythm, having biked over and stayed for tea - again - when Amanda and I had planned an evening talking about boys we knew and mucking around with Amanda's new 'Nice Nails' kit to make up for the fact that we were the only girls in the entire class not going to Kerry Palmer's Slumber Party that night.

Except, of course, for Stacy Morgan.

"When I'm famous," Stacy was saying, and Amanda was rolling her eyes, "I think I shall wear crimson nail varnish in the evenings for all the premieres I shall attend. I can accessorize - " She paused said the word again, just for effect. "Accessorize with glossy lipstick to match." She looked at her red nails. "I think crimson's so stylish, don't you, Sammy?"

Considering I'd just painted my nails Sparkly Blue and Amanda was in the process of painting hers Glittering Green, I didn't reply. Not that Stacy would've heard me. She'd gone all dreamy-eyed.

"I shall have long blonde hair swept up on top and I shall go to casinos with gorgeous dark haired guys who wear tuxedos."

"Tuxedos! You've been watching too many James Bond movies," Amanda muttered.

"Casinos are to do with gambling," I said, "The minister at our church said gambling's about hoping to get something for nothing and generally losing a lot of money in the process."

Stacy twitched her nose, bit her lip and clicked

her heels. "It's all right," she said, with her rather goofy smile, "I shan't bet. I'll just stand there looking glamorous."

The very thought of this toothy twit who had her straggly fair hair drawn back tightly from her forehead with two old fashioned brown clips looking glamorous suddenly made me burst into giggles but I turned them into a cough.

"Oh, it'll be a wonderful, glamour-filled life. But I may have to work in rep first."

Amanda frowned. "Why're you talking about being a sales rep? All you ever go on about is acting."

Stacy smirked a superior smirk. "Repertory theatre. The fringe."

Amanda's pretty face registered a complete blank. Stacy didn't notice. Her eyes were shining. "I shall have a mansion in Los Angeles with a heart-shaped swimming pool. I can just see myself at twenty. By that time I shall have been in at least one Soap. Or maybe a musical."

"Oh Lord!" I prayed, silently, remembering the squeaky voice I'd heard in the part of Drama class that our teacher called Musical Expression, "Please don't let her start singing!"

Amanda obviously had the same thought, because she looked horrified and said, quickly, "How do you see yourself at twenty, Sammy?"

"Eh? Oh. College, I suppose."

"Going to some beautiful old university with dreaming spires, sitting in a dusty room full of books, discussing life and the infinite cosmos with a knowledgeable old sage!" sighed Stacy, "Can I use your loo?"

11

"Is she for real?" said Amanda, as Stacy bolted the bathroom door.

"Hardly!"

"Do you really see yourself sitting in a dusty old room discussing life with a - what did she call him?"

"A sage."

"I thought that was something you stuffed chickens with."

"Different sort of sage. She means a wise old man. Hmm. Sometimes I'd rather take off round the world in a horse and caravan with a couple of dogs meeting lots of different people and seeing lots of different places."

"Los Angeles!" said Amanda, in a rather cruel imitation of Stacy's voice.

"Actually, I quite fancy Devon. Or Cornwall."

"How romantic!" Amanda was still doing Stacy's accent, and we both sniggered rather horribly. Stacy pulled the flush - which, since Mum had got it fixed, sounded like a jet plane coming in to land - and we tried to keep straight faces as she walked back into the room.

"I shall most certainly have really plush lavatory paper when I'm famous," she said, "And I shall come and visit you at college, Sammy."

"With a supply of loo paper?" I raised my eyebrows. "Thanks!"

"Anyway, she's changed her mind." Amanda scrutinised her nails, "She's going to buy a horse and go travelling instead."

"Oh." Stacy put on her most gormless expression. "Kerry Palmer's got a horse, hasn't she?"

"A pony," Amanda sounded glum.

"Called Russett," I added.

Amanda and I fell silent now we were reminded that we weren't at Kerry's party. She lived in a big house called Newlands and had her own red brick stable and a field ringed by oak trees. And her parties were excellent. Once, her mum had hired a real beautician to come and give advice on cosmetics but my mum was furious about it because I'd only been eleven and she said that was far too young to think about make-up. But that wasn't the reason I wasn't at Kerry's party that night.

It was October 31st.

Kerry's party had a Halloween theme. Everyone had to turn up dressed as a ghoul or a witch or a ghost and they were going trick-or-treating before having a party and watching the video 'Night of Terror' and telling spooky stories. Kerry had said there'd be fireworks and I thought, there will be when I tell my mum.

But there hadn't. Because I was clever.

I'd told Mum about the party when her new boss, Alex, was giving us a lift home from somewhere. I knew she wouldn't blow her top in front of him; she had been noticeably more relaxed about life since she'd gone to work for Alex, who was a Christian. Quite a nice man actually and one who was really enthusiastic about God. I had a sneaking feeling Mum rather admired him.

So when I said, "Oh by the way, Mum, I've been invited to a Halloween party and trick or treating and scary video Sleepover at Kerry's," she didn't respond by bursting into flames and saying such a thing would only occur over her dead body. Instead she looked at

13

Alex, swallowed a bit and said, "Well, to be honest, I don't think that's a very good idea - do you? Maybe we ought to - er - have a discussion about the reasons I'd prefer you not to go - at home - later?"

I suppose I hadn't seriously thought my mum would agree to it, however more relaxed about life she was feeling. But it had been worth mentioning, just in case. I had sighed loudly, imagining quite a heated 'discussion' and knowing for sure I could kiss Kerry's party goodbye. I'd felt a little resentful, unwrapped some chewing gum and wondered where to stick the wrapper in Alex's immaculate new car.

"Hmm, a Halloween party," Alex had said.

"Everyone in my class is going," I'd mumbled, "Well - all the girls."

"You really want to go, Samantha?"

I'd shrugged.

"Alex," began Mum, "I really think Sam - "

"I was just thinking," said Alex, "How old are you, Samantha? Thirteen? You gave your life to Jesus not long ago, isn't that right?"

"Yeah."

"Funny - I was thirteen when I asked Jesus into my life, too. D'you know, not long after, someone asked me to go and see a horror film with them. Know what I did? Before I agreed to go, I checked it with Jesus. I figured he knew best what was good for me and I'd do what he said - after all, I'd given my whole life to him."

"Yeah?"

"Yep. I've always found that's the best way to do things. See what he says, first."

"You mean I ought to ask Jesus about this party?"

Alex had winked at me in the driver's mirror, "That's it. Ask Jesus."

"OK." I'd sat back. "I will."

Mum had opened her mouth but she seemed to catch Alex's eye. I noticed Alex smile reassuringly at my mum and she kept quiet - although I could tell she was just bursting to say something. I'd felt quite good all of a sudden, as if I was being trusted at last with some responsibility in my own life. In fact, I'd felt quite grown up.

Later, I'd done as Alex suggested, and as I'd prayed I'd felt the total assurance that Jesus didn't want me to go and take part in something which glorified dark and horrid things and then watch a nightmare video which would probably scare me to death. After all, as my mum often said, Jesus came to set us free from fear. So I'd told Mum and she looked incredibly relieved and breathed "Praise the Lord!" and Alex - who was having a cup of tea in our kitchen at the time - grinned and said that Jesus had told him the same sort of thing about the movie he'd been invited to years ago.

Next day, feeling a bit like a noble martyr, I boldly told Kerry and the rest of the class. They thought I was very strange indeed. Amanda stuck by me and said if I wasn't going, neither would she. Stacy said she wouldn't go either. But then, she didn't have much choice because she hadn't been invited.

And that's how they both wound up in my bedroom that night. Mum was so glad I'd decided for myself that I wasn't going to the party that she didn't object to us messing around with the Nail Kit although I knew she didn't like painted nails 'on children'; she

15

just said we could 'play at it' if we wanted, but that I must be sure to 'wipe that stuff off' before I ventured anywhere near the front door.

"You know," said Stacy, "I'm pleased I chose not to go to the party."

"You chose!" I spluttered.

"Uhuh. I mean, what's Halloween anyway? Just a lot of dressing up as ugly, evil things, and for what reason? It's preposterous."

"I'd have thought you liked dressing up," remarked Amanda, "You wanting to be an actress."

"Oh yes, if the part demands it, but that's quite, quite different. I mean, I'd dress up for a play, if we were to put one on."

All of a sudden, it looked as if someone had switched a light on in Stacy's brain.

"A play!" she repeated, and her face lit up in excitement.

And that's how it all began.

Stacy's Idea

"All right," said Stacy, "Which one are we going to do?"

"What?"

"Which play?"

I groaned.

"Stacy, we are not going to do a play!" Amanda stuck her fork aggressively into her salad.

The noise of students and teachers chattering and clattering their cutlery as they ate their lunch drowned out what Stacy said next but she didn't seem to want a reply, she just sat back in her seat, her baked potato going cold, and stared into space, her usually wan cheeks pink and glowing.

"If we don't ditch her soon," whispered Amanda, "I'm going to go crazy."

Some of the kids at the next table were giggling. One of them - a big, bullish sort of girl called Trina Finch - had seen Stacy's little round eyes and slack jaw gawping at the ceiling and found it funny enough to nudge the others and start laughing.

"Stacy! Stacy!" I tweaked her elbow.

"What? Oh - I was just dreaming."

"Well, try shutting your mouth when you do it. You look dopey." I tucked into my chips and tried to ignore the tittering still going on at the next table.

"I could be Lady Macbeth...Ophelia...I could be Desdemona!"

"You could be murdered," I said, "If Trina Finch

gets her hands on you."

Stacy leaned forward, earnestly. "We could put on a Christmas play!"

"Look, Stacy, why don't you talk to Miss Grieves about it?" I pointed towards the Drama teacher who was sitting at a table a little way away. "She runs the school drama club."

Stacy ate a little of a her baked potato and shook her head.

It was a while before she admitted that she'd already tried Miss Grieves but although she'd read for a part in the Christmas production of the musical 'The Christmas Heist' which was going to be performed at our school's annual Winter Gala for parents and kids, she was told she could only have a non-singing part as a Christmas tree.

"My singing voice isn't quite as strong as it might be," she said, "It's something I shall have to work on at Stage School."

"Well, that's it then," said Amanda, "You're a tree. Now, let's drop the subject of silly plays. You've been on about it for nearly a whole week and it's boring."

"I shall, of course, throw myself whole-heartedly into my part as a tree. I shall be a Christmas tree. It's just that I'd like - "

Amanda had had enough. "Sammy! Guess what? You remember Tank Willis, who I went out with a little while ago? He asked me out again this morning."

"But you finished with him!"

"I know. What a cheek!"

"You look pleased, though."

"Well, it's quite flattering."

"He's horrible."

"Yes, there is that."

My friend shook back her curtain of blonde hair and I wished for the millionth time that I was as pretty as she was. But I wasn't. I hadn't even had a boyfriend yet - although I quite admired one of the boys at the youth club I went to, and thought he liked me, as well.

I really liked Parkside Youth Club, too. It was attached to the big lively church where Mum's boss Alex worshipped. There were a whole group of kids of my age there who were Christians. When I went there I didn't feel quite so isolated and odd because I knew I wasn't the only teenage Christian in the world.

Ivy Street, the church where Mum and I went, only had a youth club for younger children and I'd stopped going there several weeks ago when I joined Parkside. Actually, I thought we ought to go to Parkside Church (or Parkside Christian Fellowship as it was officially known) rather than Ivy Street because it was a lot more exciting and they had keyboards, drums and clapping and dancing whereas all we had at Ivy Street was a bald-headed minister called Mr Skinner who was also a postman. Then of course there was the ongoing argument between two factions in the church - one lot who wanted to liven things up, and one lot who didn't. This meant that one week it was quite a lively service with stuff like modern(ish) jolly songs and open prayers where anyone could join in if they had the nerve. Then the next week we'd have what they called a Traditional Service usually led by a severe-faced old deacon called Maurice Watt, where we sang ancient hymns full of Thees and Thous. Mum said these hymns were packed full of theological

19

soundness but the trouble was I didn't understand the words. With all this going on, church could be quite confusing. No wonder Mr Skinner always looked nervous.

Actually, Mr Skinner was a lot more nervous than usual because he was running the kids' youth club as well as visiting the sick and giving sermons and doing all the things he usually did (and, of course, delivering letters). This was because the youth leader - Bouncing Bob, as I called him - was on some sort of Christian Crusade for three months, spreading the good news about Jesus abroad. The Crusade was a Tent Mission run by a famous evangelist. You know the type. They usually turn up at your church and preach in a booming voice. However, seriously, some people who come to hear the booming voice actually hear about Jesus for the first time and then ask him into their lives. God shows them that Jesus really died on the cross for them, taking all the punishment they deserved for their sin and wrong-doings. And by the way this was what had happened to me recently. Anyway, Bob had gone off to somewhere very warm and pleasant with white sandy beaches, and wasn't expected back till sometime in late January.

I got the phone call from Mr Skinner that Thursday evening just as I was eating my tea.

Or rather, my mum did.

"What? Aha....hmm...oh yes, minister. No problem. She'll be delighted - that's if she's finished her homework. Have you finished your homework, Sam?"

"Eh?"

"Homework!" she hissed, putting her hand over

the mouthpiece, "Have you done it?"

"Why?"

"For goodness' sake! Just say yes or no!"

"Yes, I've done it," I admitted, cautiously, "Why, Mum?"

"She'll be along later!" Mum said into the receiver, and put the phone down. She came back to the table and dug into her tagliatelli. "It was Mr Skinner. He'd like you to help him with the children tonight at the club."

"Oh Mum!"

"What's the matter? You like them, don't you! He specifically said to ask you because you were so good with them and he's having a few problems. I thought you'd feel honoured."

I didn't. I felt annoyed because she'd accepted on my behalf without asking me first. I didn't much want to play idiotic games with a load of kids when I'd rather have watched TV. Then I realised something. Stacy had invited herself round again this evening. At least I'd get away from her bleating for a change.

"Oh well," I said, "It's cool, I suppose. I'd better ring Stacy and tell her I'm going out."

"Poor Stacy! Sam, you can take her with you to the youth club."

"Oh no!"

"You could ask her if she'd like to go with you to Parkside on Fridays, too - she'll be meeting Christians of her own age. That's if you haven't already mentioned it to her?"

"Mum!" I sat back, exasperated.

"What's the matter?"

I decided to be frank. "Mum, really and truly, I

don't like Stacy Morgan!"

"Don't be silly!"

"Mum, I'm not being silly. I don't like Stacy, I've put up with her because you said I ought to show her Jesus and stuff, and I've tried to be nice, but she is just so stupid!"

"Samantha!"

"Honestly, I've got to get away from her sometimes! And I love Parkside, and I really don't want her hanging around me there!"

"That's rather a selfish attitude. I'm surprised at you, Sam."

She put on her disapproving mother expression and ate her meal in silence. I pushed my plate away, not hungry anymore.

We still weren't speaking when I went out later on. With Stacy in tow, of course, saying she hoped we didn't have to rush about too much in wild games and get all hot and sweaty.

I stopped and put some chewing gum in my mouth. I felt grumpy. It had started to rain.

"Look, Stacy. You don't have to come, you know. You could go home."

"Oh no, that's preposterous. I'll come," she trilled, "Got to keep you company!"

"Huh. Don't your parents ever miss you? You're round my place practically every night!"

"No, they don't miss me." Her voice wasn't all frilly and twittery like usual. It was gloomy. And it suddenly struck me that she never ever invited me back to her house. I wondered why. But I wasn't interested enough to think much more about it.

"All right," I pushed open the church hall doors,

and the bright light blazed out onto the wet street, "But you will have to get hot and bothered. They like mad games."

"Samantha! At last!"

Mr Skinner emerged from a group of yelling kids. He was flushed in the face and his tie was askew. As he clasped his hands together I thought how much he reminded me of the hero in an incredibly boring old film my mum had made me watch because she said it was a true historical account. This hero had been defending some dreary old fort in the desert and everyone else had been killed by bandits, and just as everything was looking pretty bleak, a load of soldiers had turned up and saved his life. He had looked at the soldiers in much the same way as Mr Skinner was looking at me now, but I resisted the temptation to point out the similarity in expressions and just said, "hello," before nodding at my companion, rather ungraciously. "You know Stacy, Mr Skinner."

"Ah - yes!" Mr Skinner blinked at her and Stacy turned on a mega-watt smile I noticed she reserved for adults. "How good of you to give up your precious time to come and help us!"

I was about to say it was all right, but Stacy got there first.

"Oh, we're just glad to be here. Aren't we, Sammy?"

"Sammy's here! Hooray!" shouted some of the kids.

"Truth is, I don't know what to do with them!" Mr Skinner mumbled, mopping his brow with a big white handkerchief, "Youth leadership is a gift and I'm afraid I haven't been blessed in this department! I

23

don't suppose you've got any ideas, Samantha? I mean, Bob always said you were an asset to the club because you were good with them, and they do like you, and I thought, maybe you had some ideas to keep them - er - amused? They're - bless them - like a pack of wild hyenas - "

"Sammy!" shrieked the kids, "Let's have a game!"

"Er - OK! Oi! Stop that! You're pulling my arm off! Is Dinah here?" I spotted a skinny girl waving at the back of the crowd, "Great! Dinah, get them into teams of four." I turned to Mr Skinner. "You'll have to think up a holy bit for the end. Bob used to call it his 'God Slot'."

"Yes, I can do that!" Mr Skinner looked so relieved I thought he was going to embrace me.

I was so busy organising the game and getting rid of some of the kids' boisterous energy so they'd listen to Mr Skinner's talk that I lost track of Stacy. Eventually I glimpsed her, perched on the edge of the stage, clicking her heels together and chatting to Mr Skinner, who was sitting with her, feverishly leafing through a big black Bible. Unlike me, Stacy wasn't out of breath. She wasn't messy. And I felt intensely irritated by that.

"Stacy, do you want to help out?"

"No, you're doing just fine on your own, Sammy!" she called back, "You're an inspiration!"

I said a few words under my breath that Mr Skinner would have been shocked to hear. I quickly said sorry to God and tried to swallow down the feelings of annoyance that swept over me every time I glanced in Stacy's direction. Older people seemed to find her charming, even if young people thought she was maddening. When I looked over at the stage again, she was gushing enthusiastically about something, waving her arms about, and pointing to the dull grey curtains on the stage. Mr Skinner appeared utterly entranced.

The kids and I all collapsed in a heap ten minutes later, exhausted. Then the minister stepped over us, beaming and waving his Bible, and the kids, lolling about with their tongues out, gawped up at him, too tired to be silly or ask daft questions when he talked about God.

"Children!" he said, "Something marvellous has happened!"

He nodded towards Stacy, who smiled not very modestly. I had a feeling of foreboding, and my feelings of impending doom proved right when it soon became apparent that a small part as a Christmas tree in 'The Christmas Heist' hadn't done anything to assuage Stacy's theatrical urge to star.

Mr Skinner grinned at us all.

"Children! How would you like to - wait for it - how would you like to put on a play for Christmas?"

That Girl Again

"You know your trouble," said Amanda, "You just can't say 'no'."

We were in Charlie's Cafe which was small and cramped with old fashioned fuzzy wallpaper but had a great view of Millstead high street, so you could see exactly who was out and about and what they were doing and they couldn't see you. It was a good place to sit on a rainy Saturday afternoon.

"What a nerve! I can say 'no'! I told Mum I wasn't going to take Stacy to Parkside and I didn't."

Amanda looked unbelieving as she finished her coke.

"OK, so Mum's not speaking to me. Much. But I don't care. I absolutely refuse to take that - that - girl to Parkside. I just will not look a complete idiot in front of Tim."

My friend's eyes lit up. "Tim! When am I going to meet this wonderful boy? You're always talking about him!"

I squirmed a bit. Actually, I was rather pleased that Amanda didn't show any real interest in going to a Christian youth club, for the self-centred reason that she was so stunningly gorgeous I didn't want to introduce her to Timothy Aldridge Watson. I had a nasty feeling he'd think she was a lot more attractive than awkward old Samantha Jones with her spots and wild hair. And, of course, she was.

Tim didn't go to our school. He went to St Giles

Grammar School for Boys and was incredibly clever. I thought he was marvellous. Unfortunately, he had a slight tendency to believe the same. He was good looking, with a square face and warm hazel eyes, and he liked the bands The View, and Noxide, and wanted to be a marine biologist one day. Best of all, he really did believe in Jesus.

"Oh, he's just a boy," I said, as casually as possible, unwrapping a stick of chewing gum.

"Just a boy? Really? "

"Yes, really. He's just a boy. Nobody special. Dinah's brother."

"I didn't know that! You never said." Amanda leaned forward, amazed. "Dinah! I've got the right Dinah, have I? That thin kid who's always getting beaten up at school by Trina Finch and her sister for going on about God?"

"She's not always being beaten up! It was just the once, and we rescued her. Remember? She's a bit - well - "

"A bit like a religious maniac."

"She isn't. She's a Christian, like me."

"Yeah, but you're not always on about it, ramming it down people's throats."

I felt indignant on Dinah's behalf. "She doesn't do that. She's just - er - fervent."

"Fer - what? D'you get that word from Soppy Stacy?" Amanda checked her expensive watch. "Oh! Quick! Finish your coke - we're going to miss our bus!"

We very nearly did and had to race to catch it. I didn't mind so much, but Amanda, who didn't run anymore because she thought it didn't look very grown-up, was annoyed all the way home and spent the journey checking her make-up in her little hand-held mirror.

We got off the bus when we reached our estate, and Amanda was even more annoyed. It was raining really hard now and her beautiful naturally corn coloured hair was getting wet and stringy. We mumbled our goodbyes and I headed for my house in Wingold Way.

Alex's car was parked outside.

It occurred to me that Alex's car was parked outside our home quite a lot.

I went in the back door, and in the kitchen were a whole band of people: Mum, dressed in a black polo neck jumper I hadn't seen before and which made her look almost attractive; Alex, drinking coffee; Mrs Kettle, our neighbour, looking plump and fussy and over made-up as usual, and -

"Stacy!"

"Oh, hello, Sammy! We were all wondering when you'd get home!"

"I didn't see your bike outside!" If I had, I may have turned round and gone off somewhere - anywhere.

"I walked over today!"

I was just about to ask her if she was actually thinking of moving in anytime soon, because I could quite easily pack up and go and live with Amanda, when Mum handed me a plate of my favourite biscuits and I instantly forgot what I was going to say.

"Coffee, Sam?" said Mum.

"Mmmmfff," I replied, with a mouthful of chocolate digestive.

"I hear you're getting into amateur dramatics,

dear!" Mrs Kettle said, with one of her wide false-teeth smiles.

Of course! Both Mrs Kettle and Alex were members of the local amateur dramatic society. I glanced at them and then at Stacy as I swallowed my biscuit. Stacy smiled in a sickly fashion and I felt out-numbered by theatrical types.

"Amateur dramatics? No."

"Oh, but you are, according to this young lady!"

I glared at Stacy. I was really beginning to feel that this obnoxious person was taking over my life and decided to reclaim some of it.

I let out a rather disparaging laugh as Mum handed me a big mug of coffee.

"Oh! That! You mean the thing the little kids are putting on at church? Amateur dramatics! Ha ha! Hardly!" I enjoyed seeing a slightly squashed expression on Stacy's face.

"We got the impression that the minister had asked you and Stacy to do some sort of Christmas drama," said Mum, looking slightly confused.

"Christmas drama! Oh Stacy, you must've mis-heard what Mr Skinner was saying." I smiled at her in mock sympathy, as if she were a bit of a twit - which, of course, I thought she was. "He just wants us to help out with the kiddies' Christmas nativity! I suppose he thought because Bob's not around there wouldn't be one this year. Just a handful of little kids dressing up as angels with tinsel halos and shepherds with old tea towels on their heads singing a few carols! And I'll tell you what, Stacy, if you pick Rowena Taylor as Mary you'll never get any of the boys wanting to be Joseph. I had to be him last year and

I'm not doing it again. That beard made me feel itchy for days afterwards!"

Stacy looked completely crestfallen. As I warmed my hands on my mug, I felt intensely satisfied, as if I'd won a huge victory. I couldn't wait to tell Amanda.

"I think," said Alex, slowly, "We're all missing the point a bit here."

"How do you mean?" I had a sinking feeling as he spoke again.

"Well, Christmas is such a brilliant time to tell others about Jesus, isn't it? Lots of people who don't usually go to church do tend to drop in. If the children put on a good show, it might get even more folk interested in the real message of Christmas - that God sent his Son into the world to save us and give us new, clean hearts and lives."

"Yes, you're right," said Mum, impressed.

"It sounds as if - from what Stacy was saying earlier - your minister might be open to something a little more ambitious than the usual nativity play. Don't you think so, Sammy? Maybe you should take advantage of that." Alex looked thoughtful. "I mean, you could always have a traditional thing, but put a different spin on it; make it a bit different, somehow. Really use this as an opportunity to tell people about Jesus."

"A Biblical epic!" Stacy's eyes were shining now. "I could be Salome, dancing before the King!"

"Well, to be honest, Stacy, I think you're probably still looking at a Christmas theme," said Alex.

"Angels and shepherds," I muttered, "old tea towels!"

"Yes, angels and shepherds and Mary and Joseph

30

and the wise men," nodded Alex, "but perhaps something else too. Maybe you could involve some of the older people."

I spluttered into my mug as I tried to imagine some of the really ancient members of Ivy Street, like Maurice Watt for instance, dressed up as angels.

"I mean older kids," said Alex, "your age."

"There's only me - and Stacy, when she comes. Which isn't every week." And I didn't add 'thank goodness' like I wanted to.

"Sam's right," said Mum, "I'm afraid they're the only teens in the church." She went into a lot of dreary explanation about how much of the congregation was pretty elderly - over forty - and most of the young kids who went to the youth club had parents who didn't go to Ivy Street chapel. "Actually," she said, "Most of the kids are unchurched," which she explained to me later meant that their families never went to any kind of church - which was a relief, because I'd had a nasty feeling that unchurched might be a subtle way of saying weird.

"All the more reason to make this play a resounding success!" Alex winked at my mum. "Get the parents in to watch the kiddies and zap them with the gospel!"

Alex grinned at me and my heart skipped a beat. He didn't mean I'd have to get up and preach or anything, did he? I wasn't going to do that - I was no T.V. evangelist - no way!

"Oh dear," sniffed Mrs Kettle, who wasn't a Christian, "I quite like seeing the little darlings dressed up. They look so sweet! But, you don't want to make Christmas too religious, do you?"

Alex didn't seem to know what to say and gaped a bit like a goldfish.

"Oh!" twittered Stacy, "It's so thrilling! Isn't it, Sammy?"

"No," I said.

"You'll have to get going with the rehearsals pretty quick, I'd say!" said Mrs Kettle.

"That's true!" Alex had recovered from his fishy moment now. "You'll want to have a meeting of all the people who are going to be involved."

"There'll be costumes needed," said Mrs Kettle, "and props!"

I was going to mutter that a bit of tinsel and tea-towels and a make-shift cradle and doll for the baby Jesus would probably do. But Alex was saying, "most importantly, you'll want a script."

"Oh!" Stacy got up so quickly she nearly knocked over her chair, "Oh, I can't sit still!"

"I get like that," I said, "usually when I've drunk too much coke."

"But I just want to begin! Get things organised!"

"Organising children! That's something Sam's good at!" said Mum.

There was a sudden silence. They were all looking at me. I stared back, feeling defensive.

"Sammy!" Stacy said, "You can be the producer! The director!"

"What! No way. I'm not into theatrics the way you are, Stacy!"

"Well, I can't do it," said Stacy, with one of her modest smiles, "I'm no use at that sort of thing. I'm an actress, not a producer or anything. Although I do intend to marry one."

I was still trying to work out who on earth Stacy planned to marry and who on earth would have her when Mrs Kettle butted in with, "Alex, you could help a bit, surely? You wrote and directed 'Murder in the Supermarket' last year. That terrible moment when the killer pounces over the frozen peas. Superb."

"Alex! Did you really write it?" Mum sounded breathless.

"Well, yes. Actually, I might be able to help. I've got this little idea - had it last year - made a few notes. Perhaps I can talk to your Mr Skinner about it."

"Oh, this is so exciting!" chirruped Stacy, "Oh! Sammy! I can't wait -".

I felt as if these people were hijacking my life.

"I'm going upstairs," I mumbled.

I stalked off, leaving behind Stacy's high pitched excitement and wondered how I'd managed to get caught up in something I really didn't want to get involved in. How could I get out of it? There had to be a way.

Then, just as I thought things couldn't get any more depressing, they did.

The telephone rang. It was my Aunty Ann, sounding neurotic as usual. She wanted to know if my ghastly cousin Kendra could come and stay with us for a while. And whilst every nerve ending in my body shrieked "No!" my mum, of course, said we'd be delighted to have her.

As I crept away to my bedroom I wondered at how life could be reasonably OK one moment and a total nightmare the next.

Whelks and Cosmic Wanderers

I've often thought how amazing it is that when you're all dressed up in fantastic clothes the boy of your dreams never walks past, but when you're looking awful or doing something embarrassing he just turns up and says hello. Which is what happened to me that Monday.

Our school was pretty strict about pupils leaving the premises during lunch-time, but that day, Amanda had permission because she was on an errand, and of course, she had to have a friend to help her. That's how I came to be sitting on a low wall outside the row of shops on Wickham Road, watching the traffic go by, whilst Amanda bought some special grape juice in the health food shop for one of our teachers who was pregnant and having odd cravings.

I looked even more scruffy than usual. I didn't seem to be able to keep my shirt tucked into my skirt for long, and that afternoon I wasn't bothering to do anything about it because I was brooding over the fact that my cousin Kendra was turning up later on. I was wondering if it was possible for me to emigrate in the next few hours.

"Aren't food cravings disgusting!" Amanda plonked herself next to me, and poked about in the plastic bag she was holding.

"Eh? I dunno. Grape juice isn't so bad."

"I'm not talking about the grape juice." She handed me a Scotch egg and a small portion of whelks and pulled a face.

"Amanda, I like Scotch eggs and whelks."

"Ugh! Disgusting!"

That's when I heard Tim's voice.

"Hello! Sammy! It is you, isn't it!"

I nearly fell off the wall as two boys in the smart black jackets of St Giles Grammar School for Boys walked up to us.

"Tim!" I mumbled, along with a few other things, as I panicked about disposing of the Scotch egg and whelks - after all, they hardly projected the sort of cool image I was always trying to cultivate around Tim.

"Tim?" Amanda's eyes widened.

"Whelks!" I whimpered.

"Oh, give 'em here!" she grabbed the whelks and I shoved the remains of the Scotch egg into the plastic bag with the grape juice.

"Tim!" I said, again, trying to sound cool whilst frantically tucking my shirt in.

"Hey!" he said, and I sighed. He really was handsome.

"This is Amanda." I groaned, inwardly, and rather nastily, because she was such a good friend to me but I really didn't want Tim fancying her. And most boys did, because she was so striking.

"Are those whelks? Oh, great!" Tim took a few from the carton Amanda was now holding, "I love seafood."

"They're mine!" I snatched the whelks from Amanda.

"Oh, cool!" Tim sat down next to me. "Something else we've got in common, Sammy!"

35

I felt my confidence soar. He wasn't going goggle-eyed with awe in the presence of my beautiful friend. He wanted to talk to me! I was so overcome I felt a bit giddy.

"You know David?" He nodded at his friend.

"Er - yeah." I clutched the wall and wondered if my heart was all right because it was banging away in my chest so loudly. "Hey, David." I'd seen him at Parkside. He was very tall and skinny with glasses and didn't say a lot so nobody took much notice of him. He looked at me, went red, and said nothing. But I didn't care because it wasn't David I was thinking about.

"What're you doing here, Tim?"

"Half day. We decided to walk home. Well, to David's. He's got this fabulous new computer."

"Great!" I wished I could think of something more intelligent to say. But my brains had gone a bit mushy and it took me some time to get my thoughts together; Tim was sitting so close.

"Do you want to come?" Tim asked, "They could, couldn't they, David?

"Hmmph," said David, going red again, taking his glasses off, and putting them back on.

"We can't," Amanda got off the wall. "We've got to get back to school."

Tim ignored her and took some more whelks. "Sammy, what's all this about a play? My sister's got to go to some sort of meeting tomorrow evening because her youth club are going to put on a Christmas drama - she said you're in it."

"I'm not!"

Tim raised his eyebrows at my curt response.

"It's only a Christmas nativity thing," I explained, and added firmly, "But I'm not involved. I'm really busy just now. I've got my cousin coming to stay. And there's all this schoolwork. I've got a huge project on Hawaii to finish."

Tim looked a bit disappointed. "Oh. So you won't be at the meeting, then?"

"What? Oh no. Shouldn't think so." I added in my mind, not likely! No way! Not ever! No, no, no! I'd resolved not to be roped into this thing. I'd resolved it in bed on Saturday night as I lay awake steaming about how my life seemed to be heading out of control.

"Well, that's a shame." Tim stood up. "I thought we could have a bit of a laugh. Never mind."

"Eh? What? What d'you mean, 'we'?"

"My dad's got a friend called Alex. He was talking about it - the play I mean. He asked Dad if I'd be interested in helping out."

"Oh!"

"I suppose you've got a sudden interest in this silly play now," said Amanda, as we walked back to school.

"Well, it looks a bit more interesting than it did."

"I'll bet." She sniggered. Then her face straightened. "Mind you, I don't know what you see in that Tim really. He isn't that good looking you know."

"You're only saying that because he didn't take any notice of you!"

Amanda tossed her hair and didn't talk to me again until she'd given the grape juice to the pregnant teacher who asked why it was covered in Scotch egg.

I didn't have much time to dwell on my change

of heart regarding the meeting, because I had a rough time that afternoon in geography due to my terrible map of the Hawaiian Islands. I was still smarting from the accusation from the geography teacher that my map was, 'Rather like you, Samantha Jones, shambolic', when I got off the bus and headed home.

An unfamiliar car was parked in our driveway. It was a really ancient black Mini with a dent in the right wing. I hadn't got any idea whose it was, but I should've guessed it was something to do with my weird Aunty Ann because someone had painted a rather pathetic red heart over the dent and scrawled 'Love' on it, in what looked like black felt tip pen.

I realised who it was as soon as I stepped through the back door. I could hear my aunt's faintly hysterical voice in the sitting room. My heart sank down into my shoes. I was hoping they weren't going to arrive until bed-time so I could postpone having to deal with Kendra.

Then I heard a deep male voice.

"Yeah, well, like, that was just a wrong turn. You know, you make wrong turns on the road of life, and Noleen Riley from the bakery was one of them, Ann."

I pushed open the sitting room door. There was Mum, looking uneasy, and Aunty Ann, with her long hair and even longer face, dabbing at her eyes with a piece of pink tissue. A man I didn't recognise was next to her on the sofa. "So that's the new boyfriend," I thought to myself. My cousin Kendra was in another chair, her knees looped languidly over the arm. Grudgingly, I had to admit, she did look elegant and, as usual, sophisticated. But I smirked as I reminded myself that it was mostly down to the thick make-up

Aunty Ann let her wear, and that Kendra had too big a nose to be considered truly beautiful. Today, she looked bored, an expression of weary resignation making her look a lot older than fifteen. When she saw me she actually brightened up. Then the brightness turned into a sneer as she looked me up and down.

I tucked my shirt in.

"Darling!" Aunty Ann flew at me and splattered a few kisses on my cheek, "Darling, how fine you look! How fine!" She gripped my shoulders so tightly I winced. "Bo!" She faced the man on the sofa, her iron fingers still sticking into me. "This is my niece, Samantha. We call her Sam!"

"And other things," murmured Kendra.

"Samantha!" The man on the sofa smiled. It was a rugged, attractive sort of smile for someone who was so old - he must have been at least forty. I was rather transfixed by his shoulder-length golden hair, and his tanned complexion, which showed up his too-white teeth. I thought he'd had his teeth bleached and I wasn't sure about the tan and hair colour being natural, but I suppose Mum would have said I was being sceptical.

Then I realised that Bo was still droning on, "Samantha. That's a pretty name. Hmmm, I wonder what it means? Somethin' beautiful like 'cosmic dawn', I bet. So Samantha! How you doin'?"

"Er - I'm OK, thanks."

"Do you still chew all that gum?" asked Kendra.

I had been about to take out a stick of gum as she spoke, but shoved it back into my blazer pocket.

"What? Chew gum? No, I don't, actually."

"Only I read somewhere it gives you spots," my

cousin said, creasing her eyes into a concerned smile that attempted to conceal the fact that she was being unpleasant.

I was about to say something back that wasn't concealed at all, when Bo said, "Hey, gum's pretty cool. But dried banana chips are better for you," and then there was a silence because no-one really knew how to follow that. I noticed a plate full of sandwiches on the arm of the sofa. Bo took one, bit into it, and nodded. "These sandwiches are radical, Katy."

"Oh, I do beg your pardon," said Mum, "It must be the bread."

"No, like, I mean, they're cosmic. Really cool."

I wondered why someone of Bo's age was trying to speak as if he were a teenager. A very weird teenager. I decided there must be something wrong with him so I made a point of sitting as far away from him as possible.

"It's so good of you, Katy," Aunty Ann said to Mum, "to look after Kendra for me. Bo and I really need to be alone to sort out our relationship. We're going to the sea, to walk the beaches, to talk, talk, talk, in the presence of the mighty ocean."

"Trenton-next-the-Sea," said Kendra.

Trenton! It might've been in the presence of the mighty ocean, but it was also bang next to a power station and had grotty beach huts and a rickety pier. It didn't seem a very 'cosmic' place to 'talk, talk, talk'.

"Trenton? In the middle of winter?" Mum blinked.

Bo then stood up and shouted out, "Katy, there's nothing like nature. Nature is the teacher. Nature knows about relationships. The earth, the sky, the wind, the sea. We're all part of it," then he sat down and finished his sandwich. "Just cosmic wanderers. I am the pebble on the beach, Katy. I am the seaweed. I am the squid. I am the wh -".

I thought he was going to say I am the whelk for a moment and had trouble trying to control a sudden urge to laugh.

"The whale," he said.

"Hmm," Mum narrowed her eyes, "the ocean, the beach, the seaweed, the squid and the whale. Wonderful creations of our Almighty God. Just as human beings are. Another sandwich, Bo? Or are you the lettuce as well? In which case, what do cosmic wanderers generally do for food?"

Fortunately, Bo saw the funny side of this, and told Mum her sense of humour was cosmic, but Aunty Ann just looked intense, and Kendra got up and asked to borrow the loo. When she'd left the room, Ann leaned towards my mum.

"I'm just so sorry to land her on you like this. But I couldn't let her stay at home on her own and she just would not go with Dorian to James's."

I smiled as I thought of Dorian, Kendra's brother. He was the most laid back and relaxed person I ever met, quite the opposite of Aunty Ann; I wondered if he was more like his dad, my Uncle James. I wasn't sure. Ann's family lived in Kent, whereas we were in Suffolk, and Uncle James and Aunty Ann had split up ages ago, so I didn't really know much about my uncle. I remembered him lighting fireworks when I was little, cuddling the much smaller and less glamorous Kendra, and singing along to the latest songs and getting the words wrong. I frowned. Was

Uncle James still my uncle? Was he my ex-uncle? I wasn't sure whether someone stayed your uncle if they got divorced from your blood relative. I unwrapped my stick of chewing gum thoughtfully. I'd have to ask Mum about that later.

"How long do you expect to be gone?" Mum was asking, "Kendra's welcome to stay as long as she likes, of course, but don't you worry about her schoolwork?"

"Oh no. It'll be fine. The school have set her some work because I've said she won't be back before Christmas."

Christmas! Surely Kendra wouldn't be staying that long! I nearly choked on my chewing gum and stared pleadingly at Mum. Bo must have seen the look, because he said, seriously, "You know, we can't tell how long it's going to take to align our vibes. This is our life journey, Katy. It's totally crucial to get it right."

"We've got to find the self in all this! Our own personal path!" said Ann.

"And - er - you couldn't do it at home, Ann?"

"Bo's been moved in his innermost being to go to the coast! He's so spiritual!" Ann gripped his hand as if she thought he might fly away if she didn't grab hold tightly. "And anyway," she added, "Noleen Riley was making a lot of trouble for us at home since Bo dumped - um - felt it was right to change his life path. She's a very vindictive woman, you know."

"Bad vibes. Uncool. Any more sandwiches?" said Bo.

Mum didn't say anything more. She got up, went out into the kitchen, and made some tea. Kendra came back and casually remarked to her mother that she didn't much like the thought of sleeping on the futon

42

in our spare room for very long. Bo told her a bit of hardship was the way of galactic spirituality and then checked his watch and said it was time to leave because the hotel would be expecting them. And he and Ann got up to go.

It was dark outside. The streetlamps cast a dreary yellow glow on the wet road.

"It's starting to rain," cried Aunty Ann, as if it were a cosmic sign.

"Make him drive carefully," said Kendra; I thought her voice was a bit more tremulous than usual.

Aunty Ann gripped Kendra's shoulders.

"Just think, darling! You'll have such glorious company with Sam here, all girls together!"

I tried to smile politely but inwardly just thanked God Kendra wasn't going to be at my school as well as at home.

"Now Kenny darling, if you want me, you've got your mobile," said my aunt, "Ring me anytime, darling - well, except for after seven in the evenings - and mornings might be a bit tricky. And afternoons. Oh, and I'm not taking my mobile. Ah. Never mind, darling; you'll have a lovely time without me cluttering up your vibes for a while. I know you understand how important it is for me to find out about my life journey! Take care of yourself!"

Aunty Ann gave her daughter a huge hug which Kendra stiffly returned. Then Ann got into the car with Bo and they zipped away into the night. And Kendra stood there in the driveway, watching the red tail-lights disappearing into the darkness.

Anger

"I see you haven't sorted your hair out yet," said Kendra.

"What do you mean, 'sorted it out'?"

"You look terrible with that wild mop all over your face. It looks so greasy. Don't you ever wash it?"

I was about to fire back an acid retort but suddenly felt I couldn't be bothered. I'd had a really hard day at school and I had loads of homework to do before I went to the meeting.

"Look, Kendra. If you're going to be staying here for a while, we're going to have to get on. So shut up making personal remarks about me and let's just ignore each other. OK? Otherwise I might just murder you."

She glanced out of my bedroom window. "Does that gorgeous boy still live next door?"

"What? Oh, Luce. No, he moved away, he's living with his girlfriend I think. Kendra!" I slung my schoolbag down on my bed, exasperated. "Are you listening to me?"

"It was totally boring today," she said, her eyes still fixed out of the window.

"Yeah, well, that's tough."

"Well, it is tough, if you must know, doing set work on your own. You try spending an afternoon with the Economic Reforms of 19th Century Britain without anyone to have a giggle with." I almost felt sorry for her for a moment, but she added, with a scrutinising gaze over her shoulder, "That school uniform's not very flattering, is it? Makes you look even more fat and lumpy than you really are," and my sympathetic feelings disappeared.

"Better than looking like a stick, like you do."

"Silly baby. You're just jealous because I'm slim."

"Jealous! Of you! Don't make me laugh!"

"Well, look at you. You've got tons of spots. Or are they freckles? Whatever they are, they look awful. Still, you know what they say about ugly ducklings, they blossom - eventually - into beautiful swans." For a minute, I thought she was being nice. Then she said, "Of course, in your case, it probably won't happen."

I stared at her with dislike. All that make-up plastered on her smug face! That short tight skirt showing off her long legs! Who was she trying to impress? I was about to ask her, when she said,

"Why does your mum make us go to bed at half past nine? Surely she doesn't always make you go to bed so early? You're going red. She does, doesn't she!"

I'd been hoping Mum would extend it while Kendra was with us, but she hadn't. I felt my cheeks burn with embarrassment. I felt such a kid.

"I usually stay up until at least eleven on school-days. I can go to bed anytime I like, actually. At weekends, I stay up until one or two o'clock in the morning, watching videos." Kendra sniffed. "Mind you, the kind of videos you've got aren't worth watching. All children's stuff and religion. Oh - and what's this?" Kendra's laconic gaze locked onto a small picture I had on the wall. It was somebody's idea of what Jesus looked like. He was carrying a lamp, and knocking on a door.

"'Here I am! I stand at the door and knock. If anyone hears my voice and opens the door, I will come in and eat with him, and he with me'." She eyed a line at the bottom. "Oh! 'Revelation 3:20'. It's the Bible, is it? I suppose this is meant to be Jesus, is it? Oh well. Makes a change from The View poster you used to have in here, anyway. Not that you ever had the guts to actually put it up on the wall. Your mum doesn't like bands, does she? I s'pose she likes this religious picture, though. You're a good little girl, aren't you?"

"I know you don't believe in Jesus, but I do. And this is my room. And my house."

Kendra looked at me with glacial indifference. "I couldn't care less what you believe. It's all rubbish. You only believe in it because of your mum anyway. She makes you - just like she makes you go to bed early. She'd better not try and make me believe in religion. If she does, I'll - " She seemed at a loss for words, and set her over-glossed lips in a straight line. "Well, she'd better not, anyway."

"Mum's not going to make you do anything. She wouldn't. She's not like that. And I don't believe in Jesus just because of her, either. I believe in him because I know he's real."

"He's real!" scoffed Kendra.

"Kendra! I don't need this stuff with you right now! I've got stacks of homework and then I've got to go to a meeting."

"What meeting?"

"It's none of your business. It's church stuff."

"Church, church, church! Religious nuts!"

"We're not. We just believe in -"

Kendra yawned, loudly. I began to feel very very irritated.

"Kendra, I don't want you coming into my room anytime, especially when I'm not here. Get it? Now get lost. You've only been here a day and I've already seen enough of you."

"I didn't want to come here anyway, if you must know."

"So why did you?"

She picked up a musical box that was on my window sill. "Because I hate my dad's woman." Sniffing angrily, Kendra almost spat out the last word before continuing, "That woman says untrue things about my mum. I wasn't going there."

"Oh, terrific. So we've got you."

She put the musical box back in its place. "Yes, you've got me. So terribly sorry."

"It's all right so long as you don't bother me and go away before Christmas."

I only realised how truly nasty that was as she slipped out of the room without saying anything horrible in return. I heard her lock the bathroom door. I bit my lip, and gloomily unwrapped a stick of chewing gum.

Kendra really did bring out the bad side of me, just like Stacy. Why did God allow such ghastly people to come into our lives? If they stayed out, we'd probably get on a lot better, because we wouldn't be tempted to be horrible. Why did he allow it? Why couldn't we just meet nice people? Nice people - like me.

Nice people like me! Who was I kidding? I really wanted to start my homework but my rotten words to Kendra kept swirling round my brain. I sighed. I had to pray.

I remembered what Jesus said in the Bible about the importance of praying in private, so I shut my door, and perched on the edge of my bed, my eyes closed. Then I thought - did God mind us praying when we were chewing? Probably not. Still, I couldn't take a chance, took the gum out of my mouth and chucked it in my waste paper bin.

"Hello, Jesus," I said. I stopped. It had suddenly occurred to me that I hadn't actually spoken to Jesus for a while. In fact, I couldn't remember the last time I'd really prayed - not just sent up a few words about 'Please don't let Mrs Glitchen get cross with me when I can't vault the horse in gym' or 'Please get Mum to buy me a TV for my bedroom/mobile phone/new computer'. Then it hit me; the last time I'd seriously prayed and known God's peaceful presence in my heart was when I'd asked him about going to Kerry's Halloween Sleepover.

"Oh dear," I said.

I recalled the sort of 'prayers' I used to say before I actually came to believe in Jesus, prayers that were half hearted and selfish and just thrown up haphazardly like you might cast a piece of chewing gum into a bin and hoped it hit the spot. But now I knew he was real; he was my Friend. How come I hadn't spoken properly to him lately?

"It's Stacy's fault!" I grumbled, "The stupid play! And now Kendra, and all this hassle!"

I seethed about everything for a moment.

"I don't like Stacy! And I really hate Kendra!"

A sentence popped into my brain. It was uninvited and I didn't want to hear it. It was like my mum's voice replaying something she'd said to me - that I ought to be nice to Stacy to show her by example that Jesus loved her. Yes, Jesus loved her, and I was sitting there thinking hateful thoughts about her and my cousin. But then, they were just so objectionable.

I seethed some more, felt angrier and angrier, till in the end I found it impossible to pray at all. So I did my homework and made a mess of it and felt panicky because time was rolling on and I had wanted to do something with my hair before the meeting. But just as I snapped my books shut and wondered if there was time to wash it, Mum shouted up the stairs that tea was ready, and I saw that it was six o'clock.

I shovelled my sausage and chips down my throat so quickly Kendra murmured words like 'disgusting' and 'pig' and Mum pointed out that I was very likely going to get the most appalling indigestion - which made my heart lurch, because there's nothing worse than having a problem with your digestion when you're trying to impress a boy.

So I ate the rest of my meal slowly, all the time with my eye on the clock, and then Kendra sweetly asked my mum if she could have a shower and Mum said yes which meant there was no chance of me getting into the bathroom to wash my hair or do anything to make myself look remotely attractive, which made me madder than ever.

After tea, I hammered up the stairs and put on a nice close-fitting top which Amanda had leant me, and my best jeans. Then I tried to do something with my hair, but couldn't make it look even slightly under control. It was dead straight and flopped everywhere - and it did look greasy. It wasn't quite long enough to go in a pony-tail; and anyway, my ears were too big for a pony-tail to look good. So I decided to just shove a hair-brush through it and hope for the best. Only I couldn't find my brush.

Then Kendra came out of the bathroom and stood in my bedroom doorway smelling wonderfully fragrant and looking fantastic in a baby blue sweater and ski-pants which made her legs look a thousand miles long.

"All right?" she said, dangling my hair brush casually by one of her manicured fingers and I nearly bit her as I grabbed it and shot into the bathroom. I fleetingly wondered why my cousin was getting so dolled up; I thought it was just because she always liked to look as if she was about to go to a night-club even when she was hanging around the house. So I was more than stunned when Mum tapped on the door and asked me to hurry up because she and Kendra were waiting for me, and if I didn't get a move on, we'd all be late for the meeting!

"What!" I exclaimed.

I came out of the bathroom and the first thing I saw was my mum's lips. She'd either put lipstick on or her lips were swelling up.

"You knew I was going!" she said.

"No!"

"Of course you did."

"But why, Mum?" I demanded, rudely, "You're nothing to do with all this!"

"Of course I am. I'm very interested in the play. Alex said -".

Ah! I thought. Alex!

"Alex said he wanted me to go to the meeting.

Lots of people are going."

I groaned. The thought of my mum being there, cramping my style as I tried to impress Tim! Kendra tittered.

"Coo, Sam, what're you wearing? That top's two sizes too small."

"Yes, it is," said Mum, "Where did you get it? Amanda I suppose? Change it, quickly, love."

I glared at Kendra. "Why's she going? She isn't interested in the church!"

"Samantha, Kendra's been here on her own all day. We can't leave her here alone, can we!"

"I don't see why not!"

"Samantha!"

"Well, she thinks we're all religious nuts!"

"Don't be silly!" said my cousin, coolly, "I hope I'm broad-minded enough to allow everyone to believe what they want to believe!"

"You lying little hypocrite!" I almost shouted.

"Samantha! Apologise at once!" said Mum, shocked.

"No, I won't, because she is lying. She thinks we're nuts."

"Apologise!"

Kendra, standing behind my mum, stuck her tongue out at me.

"Come on, quickly!" said Mum, "And then go and change that terrible top!"

I had a last stab at defiance. "I like this top. I'm not going to change it."

"Samantha! It's indecent. You'll change it or you won't go out tonight."

I was almost bubbling over with rage. I glared at

my cousin.

"I'm sorry!" I said, in a strangled sort of voice.

"I forgive you," she replied, "That's a Christian thing to do, isn't it, Aunty Katy?"

"Yes, Kendra. Sam! That top. Change it, now, please. Put a jumper on. Wear that fluffy one with the kittens on that Mrs Kettle knitted you. That always looks lovely."

I heard Kendra say, "Kittens! How sweet!", as I went into my room and slammed the door behind me. I truly felt as if no-one in the entire history of the world could ever have felt as angry as I did at that moment.

Ten minutes later, the three of us were setting off towards the church hall. I wasn't talking to either of them. I'd put on an old yellow sweatshirt which Mum told me looked as if it needed a wash, and Kendra said made me look ill. But it was too late to change again, and all I could think as I pushed open the church hall doors, was that it was a million times better than fluffy kittens.

The Meeting

I hadn't really thought many people would be very interested in the meeting. In truth, I hadn't actually thought much beyond what I'd say to Tim and how I could knock him out with my beauty, wit and charm, so I was surprised to see about fifteen people in the brightly lit church hall that evening.

Mr Skinner was there, flapping around. Stacy was at his side, distributing sheafs of paper, looking self-important and goofy as usual, in long white socks and a dark blue pinafore dress which made her look weird and deeply unfashionable. Which, of course, she was. Maurice Watt was there, too - which I found odd, because he'd never shown up at anything to do with the youth club before - still, there he was, solemnly fiddling with the radiators. And some ladies from the church were clucking together on hard-backed chairs that had been optimistically arranged in several rows.

Alex was standing, relaxed, hands hipped, chatting to them, and when he saw my mum he beamed and said "Katy!" She began introducing him to my cousin.

Someone whistled. I saw Tim, sitting on the stage, beckoning to me. David was with him. So was Dinah. Gladly, I slipped away from my mum and Kendra and parked myself next to Tim.

"Sam! Who's that?"

For a minute, I didn't know what he meant - and

then I realised, with a sinking feeling, that he was staring at Kendra.

"That? Oh, that's just my cousin."

I immediately regretted owning up to the fact that she and I were related.

"Your cousin!" Tim stared, disbelieving, "Wow, you don't look alike, do you!"

I crumpled, inwardly, as Tim said something to David that I didn't catch. David coughed, went red, and adjusted his glasses. It hadn't occurred to me that Tim might find my repulsive cousin attractive. I glared at her with loathing. She had her moodiest expression on, and was pouting glossily, stretching her everlasting legs out as she reclined on one of the chairs. The harsh light wasn't flattering, but she still managed to look a thousand times more glamorous than the rest of us.

"She looks like a model," said Dinah, in a slightly hushed, awestruck voice.

"A model!" I laughed, bitterly. "It's all make-up. She's got a massive nose. And," I added, hoping to put Tim off Kendra forever, "She isn't a Christian."

"Isn't she? Oh, what a shame," said Dinah.

"She looks a bit too made-up. I like girls who look natural." Tim smiled at me. I felt completely gooey - and relieved. He didn't seem to find my cousin attractive after all!

"I'm sure she's a nice person, though," said Dinah.

I stared at her, vexed. She always saw the good in people!

"Nice? She isn't!"

"Oh well. Here," Dinah handed me some typewritten papers which were clipped together, "this

54

is a copy of the play we're going to do. It's ever so good, Sammy."

"Oh?" I was trying to work out why a Christmas nativity play was entitled Lord of Time and wondering whether we'd got hold of a science fiction script instead of a Christian one, when I spotted Stacy strutting over to us.

"Oh no!" She was heading straight for me. I couldn't bear the thought of Tim seeing that I actually knew this person.

I shoved the typewritten script in front of my face and pretended to be engrossed, hoping she'd get the hint and go away. Then I felt a hand push me ever so gently - but determinedly - to one side, and before you could say 'Stacy' she was squashed between me and Tim!

"Oi!"

"Hello, Sammy! I see you've got a copy of the play. Whose is it? Here's one of your own." She snatched the script out of my hand, gave it back to Dinah, and handed me a copy with 'Sammy' written at the top in her large childish scrawl. I was beginning to feel very angry again. If this girl thought she could monopolise me all evening when I wanted to be with Tim, she was mistaken!

"Stacy," I began - but she turned away from me and began to talk to Tim. In fact, she leaned right over him, smiling her toothy smile. "Is that your copy?"

"Er - well, yeah," Tim glanced at the sheets lying behind him on the stage.

"Have you read it through?"

"Um - well, no."

"You're a very naughty boy, then, aren't you!"

She scooped up his copy, and tapped him sharply on the head with it. Tim looked stunned, and I wished I was a thousand miles away from the cringingly awful Stacy - or better still, that she was a thousand miles away, or even on a different planet or a different galaxy without any means of return.

"You know, your cousin really is fantastic looking," observed Dinah.

"Whose cousin?" asked Stacy, blankly.

"Sammy's." Dinah nodded towards Kendra, "We were just all saying, she looks like a model."

I was about to point out that we weren't all saying any such thing, but as I looked at Kendra (and I wasn't the only one staring, Stacy had fixed her round little eyes on my cousin) I thought she really did radiate glacial style, even if it was mostly down to thick foundation and black eyeliner.

Then Stacy caught my eye, smiled vacantly and said, "Which one is she? Oh - that girl in the blue jumper? I hadn't noticed her," which was a blatant lie.

"Shh!" said Dinah, "Mr Skinner is talking."

Stacy leaned forward, and so I was able to see Tim behind her back. He grinned at me, and I felt relieved that he didn't appear to be ignoring me totally or thinking me revolting because I had odd relatives and friends. I began to feel quite happy, until I heard the click click of Stacy's heels banging together, and I started thinking of all the dreadful things in the world that could happen to Stacy and wishing they'd happen right now.

Mr Skinner asked people to take their seats (which I always thought was a really daft way of saying, sit down!), bumbled through a few introductory sentences about how marvellous it was that folk had bothered to turn up on a miserable winter night, and then droned on for a while about the importance of the Christmas nativity play every year as a source of 'togetherness in the Lord, celebrating his birth'. An old lady slapped open the door at this point and said, " I ain't stoppin', I jus' wanted to give this to Edna," handed another old dear a crumpled brown paper bag, said, "Go easy on them prunes, they gives me the most terrible problems," and then shuffled off. Mr Skinner wiped his brow with the back of his hand and asked if the heating system was working properly because he was feeling jolly hot, and Maurice Watt creaked into action and checked the radiators slowly whilst people murmured boringly about whether or not it was hot or cold. Whilst this was going on, Tim and David huddled together reading the play, and then Tim announced it was "Cool," and Stacy looked so smug you'd have thought she'd written it.

Then Mr Skinner continued about previous year's Christmas offerings of the story of Mary and Joseph and baby Jesus, and Stacy, adopting her most vacant expression, clicked her heels interminably. And I fished in my jeans' pocket for some gum, and thought about exactly how to phrase my annoyance with the Toothy Twit later on. Fancy pushing in between me and Tim like that! What a cheek!

"But this year," said Mr Skinner, at last, "We're going to do something different. Well, sort of. A Christmas drama, based on the old old story of Jesus being born in a manger in a stable, and the glorious angels announcing his birth to the poor shepherds, and so forth, but we're going to add something. Something - ah - rather modern day, I suppose. To attract more customers - er, I mean, people - anyway, to get them to come and hear the message of God's love."

People nodded and said, "Good idea!" - except for Maurice Watt, who just frowned and made a note in an exercise book which was balanced on his bony knee; I noticed he kept on making notes during the meeting. Stacy leaned further and further forward as if she had something wrong with her hearing, and seemed to be hardly breathing, until Mr Skinner mentioned her name.

"Of course," said Mr Skinner, "The whole idea for this year's drama has been down to the inspiration of a very keen young actress - Miss Stacy Morgan!"

Heads turned, and Stacy put on her not very modest expression. I felt even more annoyed as I heard Tim mutter, surprised, "I didn't know it was your idea. I thought it was Sam's!"

Mr Skinner then said, "But I think I'd better leave the rest of the talking to Alex - after all, he wrote the play," and Alex - who'd been sitting next to my mum - stood up. People clapped enthusiastically, and Stacy sat back looking rather disgruntled; they hadn't clapped her. So I clapped Alex the loudest.

"Well, it's just something I knocked together," said Alex - and he really did sound modest, "I'd had the idea last year, actually, but didn't put it to any good use. Then I heard about Ivy Street church youth club wanting to put on a bit of a drama this year, and - well, hopefully, we can all pull together to glorify God in it."

58

"Amen!" said Mr Skinner, and Maurice Watt cleared his throat loudly.

Alex grinned, and slung his hands into his trouser pockets, and I thought he really was nice looking for such an oldie. "The thing is, as you'll have noticed, it is a real old fashioned nativity - about the birth of Jesus. I thought that's where the younger children could really get involved - kids love dressing up, and the mums and dads love to see it, too, and we can get a lot of folk interested in coming to watch the play purely because their children or grand-children are in it - people who maybe don't usually come to the church. If you notice, though, the speaking parts - " and here there was a rustle of paper as people looked at their scripts, and I wondered where mine had gone and then realised Stacy was sitting on it, "Are for older kids. Young people, really."

"How exciting!" said Dinah, quietly. Alex was speaking again.

"For those of you who haven't had a chance to have a good look at the play, it's about a time traveller who lands up at Jesus' birth in the stable, complete with angels and shepherds and sheep, and I might even throw in a few wise men - even though in the story they didn't turn up till later - which is the traditional bit everyone will love. But the time traveller moves on to about AD33 or so when Jesus has just been crucified - and I think we can forget, when we think of Jesus being born, that he did grow up to die for our sin - our wrong-doings - and rose again from the dead, and is alive today."

"That's true!" said Mr Skinner.

"Just how are the youth club portraying the

crucifixion?" asked Maurice Watt, snootily.

Alex laughed. "Don't worry, we're not going to have any Roman torture scenes. We'll just see Mary, the mother of Jesus, weeping gently. Page three of the script."

There was a another rustling of paper.

"Then, finally, the time traveller's home - in the present day. He - or she - meets someone who has given their life to this very same Jesus who came to save us all those years ago. And the good news about Jesus and his relevance for us here and now is complete - he's not just a baby from years and years ago, but someone who can change people's lives today. The Lord of Time! I was going to chuck in a scene about the Second Coming of Jesus to earth, but frankly, I thought that was a bit ambitious and might need a few zillion props. So that's it." Alex shrugged his shoulders. "The whole thing will only take about twenty minutes or so. We might get the little ones to sing a carol in the nativity scene. Um - any questions? Suggestions? Anything?"

Maurice Watt cleared his throat again and put on a disapproving look as he fingered the script in his hand. "Ah-ah-hem. Yes indeed. I have glanced through this - ahem - work and I do perceive a problem, which I think ought to be brought to the attention of those here gathered."

"Oh yes?" said Alex, pleasantly, "Do share," which I thought was magnanimous of him because if I'd taken the trouble to produce a play for a youth club of a church I didn't even attend, and someone had sourly said that they had a problem with it I would have shouted, "How dare you! I've toiled like mad

60

over this!" which shows, I suppose, how I still had a long way to go in my Christian life.

"Time travel!" Mr Watt peered down his thin nose and over the top of his half-glasses. "Hardly Biblical, is it!"

"No, it isn't," agreed Alex, "but it's a way we can show the people what happened, just like we're there watching events unfold. It's a tool to convey a message."

Mr Watt looked even more disapproving but everyone else said, "Good idea," and "See your point", and "Great!" and "Where's the tea?" And Mum and Edna, the old lady with the prunes, went off to the little kitchen to make some whilst the rest of the people started talking about what props would be needed, and racking their brains to remember where they'd put the props from last year's nativity, and then someone piped up "Er - just how are we going to portray time travel adequately?" which caused some scratching of heads. It was eventually decided that the time traveller would have to have some sort of item of jewellery like a big visible bracelet with which he or she apparently shot through time, and would just have to fiddle with it, and we'd have the lights flashing on and off when they were meant to be travelling.

Then Mum asked me and Dinah to help distribute the tea, and we did so, trying not to slop it out of the little chipped green cups into the little chipped green saucers. Someone produced a plate of biscuits, and when I offered them to Kendra she said, "No, but I suppose you're going to have at least five," and I said, "Shut up," which wasn't very Christian of me, but then I was absolutely sick of her.

I noticed Stacy - nattering away to Tim - who, I thought, looked as if he'd rather be talking to David. and Alex nearby. Stacy had disappeared when she could've been helping with the tea. I suppose she must have thought that giving out refreshments was beneath a wonderful thespian like her. Munching on a custard cream I looked towards Stacy and Tim and muttered, "Oh, poor boy, he needs rescuing. That awful girl!"

"Sammy!" said Stacy, and I noticed she was very flushed in her usual pallid face, "Scintillating news! I'm going to be the time traveller!"

"I'm the person she meets in the present day who knows Jesus," said Tim, trying not to sound excited, "And Alex has asked my sister to be Mary!"

Stacy clapped her hands together. "Oh, but it's all so thrilling! I can't wait to start rehearsals!" She gripped Tim's arm tightly. And in that moment, something became very clear to me indeed. She fancies him! I laughed, silently. She looked so totally ridiculous in her idiotic old fashioned clothes with her idiotic face and hair and teeth and everything. As if Tim would be interested in her! "We'll really be glorifying the Lord!" she said, fluttering her scanty eyelashes at him.

Really! I thought, scornfully, I've never heard her ever say a word about the Lord before now! She's trying to impress Tim! And then a thought struck me. Alex had asked Stacy and Tim and Dinah to be in this play - but he hadn't asked me! I tried to feel cool about it. After all, I hadn't really wanted to get involved in this production at all, had I?

" - so David, I'm sure we'll find you something to do," Alex was saying, and David said, "Well, I'm -

that is to say, I'd rather not - I'm - er - not on the stage, in front of - er - " and he blushed and adjusted his glasses so sharply he nearly poked his finger in his eye.

"Samantha! Sam! You'll be the co-organiser with me, won't you?" asked Alex, "I'll need plenty of help, and I won't be able to make all the rehearsals. So you'll be in charge of everything and everyone! OK?"

Not long ago, I'd have groaned at the very thought of having to do anything at all regarding this play. But bossing the actors around? Hmm!

I nodded, gratefully. "Yeah, Alex. All right." Because as I watched Stacy smile in her mostly sickly fashion at Tim, the thought of getting a chance to make her look even more silly than she already did - and in front of lots of people, including Tim - was very inviting indeed.

Worries

"How old is Alex?"

Kendra wandered into the kitchen and opened the fridge door.

"Eh? Alex?" I scratched my head. "I dunno. Thirty something I think."

"D'you like him?"

"What? Yeah, of course I do."

My cousin found some fresh orange juice and poured some. She didn't ask if I wanted any. She hovered about and I tried to ignore her. I was busy making notes on my script.

We'd had two rehearsals. The first one had been the most difficult. This was because Alex and I had been trying to arrange the manger scene that started the play off, which should, in theory have been easy - just getting the kids to stand around looking like a tableau, and then singing 'Away in a Manger'. But it had been a bit troublesome because one or two of the mums had come along to lend support; some of the kids consequently showed off. One burst into tears because he wanted to be a firefighter and put on a yellow helmet and he just wouldn't believe there weren't any in ancient Palestine 2000 years ago. One of the mums had then said her kid didn't want to be an angel because he thought they were girls. Mr Skinner had to patiently explain that angels weren't girls at all, but that in fact they were mighty awesome warriors of God. The kid sulked and said they wore silly dresses and sat on Christmas trees and Mr Skinner said no they didn't. Then the mother said 'George, really and truly, angels are what people become when they die', and poor old Mr Skinner had to explain that that wasn't right at all, angels were created specially by God and no way could a human being become an angel. He got his big black Bible out and the woman said she didn't want religion shoved down her throat and she and her kid went home.

The second rehearsal was less fraught and I really enjoyed it.

This was because it was just the older ones practising the main body of the play, which was the time travelling bit. Even better, Stacy had a sore throat and couldn't come, so Alex asked me to stand in for her. Although I'm not much of an actress, it was fun just reading through the lines, mainly because I was doing it with Tim.

Kendra plonked herself down at the kitchen table and stared at me. "Coo, you're just so into this play thing. How boring."

"It's not," I said. Of course, I'd originally thought it would be boring. But it was turning out to be quite exciting, working together with people I liked to produce something good. It was also taking up quite a bit of my precious spare time, and I didn't want to spend any of it talking to my cousin.

"Boring, boring, boring." Kendra yawned. "Living here is very nearly as boring as living at home with that dreary brother of mine, always sticking his nose in ancient books."

"I like Dorian."

"Yes, well, you don't have to live with him. You're

65

dead lucky, you know, being the only child."

"Lucky!" I felt indignant. Mum always said there was no such thing as 'luck'; we should say 'blessed by God'. But that wasn't what I felt uptight about. I didn't feel particularly 'lucky' in many ways. We weren't well off - I'd often thought Amanda was much more 'lucky' than me, because she had her own TV and video recorder and computer and mobile phone and just about everything else. My cousin was talking again.

"Yeah, lucky. You don't have to share anything with anyone. Not only do I have my dopey brother, worse, I've got two step-sisters. Dad's woman's kids. Didn't know that, did you?"

"Eh? No. I didn't."

"It means a load of strangers know my business. And they've got my dad."

I didn't know what to say to that, so I unwrapped some gum.

"I've had lots of step-dads too. Not that Mum has ever married any of them. I told you, you're lucky. Luckier than you know." She sniffed and her eyes narrowed. "Still. Maybe Aunty Katy'll get married again, and then you might get brothers and sisters after all, as well as a step-dad."

"What are you talking about?"

Kendra laughed. "Coo, you are just so dense." She leaned forward, resting her elbows on the table. "I'm talking about Alex. Alex and your mum. They're in love, aren't they!"

I was stunned. "In love! Don't be stupid."

Kendra smirked knowingly. "I bet your mum hasn't had a boyfriend since your dad died."

"Kendra, don't be idiotic. Alex isn't mum's

66

boyfriend. He's her boss."

"And he's round here practically every evening."

"He just drops by for a chat," I said, lamely, but I knew Kendra had seen the same growing closeness between my mum and Alex as I had - only I'd pushed it to one side of my mind. To tell you the truth I didn't want to think about it, I didn't want to think about it at all.

"He's always round here," Kendra went on, "putting up shelves. Then he stays for tea. Of course, he's a Christian, isn't he, so I s'pose he won't move in or anything. Christians don't do sex before marriage, do they?"

"What! Kendra! Don't be disgusting - my mum doesn't 'do' sex at all!"

Kendra raised her eyebrows. "How d'you feel about Alex as a step-dad?"

"Stop it! Alex isn't going to be my step-dad! Why don't you shut up? What do you know?"

"Just being realistic. Anyway, you ought to be glad. He's quite well off, isn't he? You and your mum will have more money. And I thought you said you liked him."

I did, but I didn't want him moving in! I didn't want a step-dad, not even someone as nice as Alex! Cold fingers seemed to grip my heart. I didn't want anyone replacing me in my mum's affections!

The back door burst open right then, and I forgot my worries, because Mum and Mrs Kettle came in, laden down with cloth-covered trays of wonderful smelling food.

We were hosting an evening's entertainment for new Christians, and people who weren't Christians but were just interested, which involved a light meal and watching a video called 'This New Life'. Mum had very cleverly got Mrs Kettle to agree to come, because Mrs Kettle was very good at making things like vol-au-vents, cakes and sausage rolls and people raved about her apple and mango salad, cheese dips and mouth watering salsas; I could never imagine Mrs Kettle being content with a few hard biscuits and a cup of tea out of a chipped cup. But I don't think Mum's motivation was just because Mrs Kettle was handy as a cook; Mum wanted her to meet Jesus.

"Kendra, Mrs Kettle has another couple of trays to carry, be a love and give her a hand!" said my mum, and as my cousin slipped off into the night, Mum winked at me and said, "Get her involved, then she may want to watch the video!" and I said, rather disparagingly, "She hasn't really got much of a choice, has she, Mum, it's freezing tonight and the central heating in the spare room is wonky," and Mum said I was getting very cynical.

Soon, other people began to arrive, and our small front room was packed with church folk and their guests. I glanced around the gathering and spotted Mr Skinner, but thankfully, no granite-faced Maurice Watt. Old Edna turned up with her friend, the one who'd interrupted the meeting with the prunes, and who said (as she settled herself comfortably by the fire) she wasn't stopping long. Mr Upson, a doddery little old man I sometimes visited because he really knew Jesus, and told me often that he prayed for me, was there, too, fiddling with his hearing aid so that it whistled loudly and people winced.

"Seven thirty! Time to start! Everyone here?" said

Mum.

"Mmm. Think so. I did drop an invitation into Mr and Mrs Morgan's house, but I've heard no more so I suppose they aren't interested," remarked Mr Skinner.

"Well, they've only been to the church a few times anyway," said Edna, "Although their daughter, Stacy, that dear little girl, sometimes comes to the morning service!"

Stacy? Dear little girl? I sighed rather ungraciously. Then just as the video was about to start, the doorbell rang, and I answered it. Stacy stood there.

"Oh," I said, rather rudely, "it's you."

"Not too late, am I?"

"Nearly. Did you bike over?"

"No, I've got a flat tyre so I walked."

"Oh yuk, in the dark! You didn't have to come." She pushed past me and went into the living room. "You're shivering like mad. I thought you'd got over your virus. Everyone! It's that dear little -"

"Are your parents coming, love?" asked Mum.

"Er - no," said Stacy, and mumbled something about her baby brother being sick.

"Oh!" cried Mum, "Poor baby! Not really ill, is he?"

"Eh? No. He'll be OK." Stacy sat down in my seat.

"We'll pray for the poor darling," said Mum.

"Oh no, Mrs Jones, it's kind of you, but that's preposterous. There's no need," said Stacy so breezily Mum blinked.

I had to sit on the floor like some kid, at the feet of my cousin Kendra who was snuggled into the best

69

easy chair looking as bored as ever, but apparently getting some amusement out of the fact that I was on the carpet.

Still, the video was quite good. It was fairly short, and featured a chap who was in one of the very popular soap operas who had become a Christian after living a very 'wayward' life, as he called it. The man said when he turned to Jesus, he believed the Lord did a kind of swap, took all his sins away, and gave him this clean new life. He said that Jesus was the Pearl of Greatest Price (which I'd never understood before). He said once you find something that is just so marvellous and priceless, you'd sell all you had to buy it, and Jesus was like that - he was so wonderful and loving, you just had to put him first and would give up anything and everything for him if he asked you to; even things that you'd really held dear, like ambitions that maybe didn't fit in with what God wanted for your life, or even people and relationships that weren't God's will either.

I felt a nice warm sense of God being right there with us and then a stab of guilt because I really wasn't praying and reading my Bible as much as I knew I should - and not as much as I had done when I first met Jesus. Anyway, that wasn't my fault, I told myself, that was Stacy and Kendra's. The video finished, and people murmured, and didn't know whether to clap or not. Mrs Kettle told Mr Skinner that she'd always quite fancied the man from the soap opera. Mr Skinner got to his feet so quickly he had a dizzy spell and had to recover for a moment before asking if anyone had any questions they'd like to ask.

"Yes," said Edna.

"Jolly good!" Mr Skinner nodded, and you could just see he was trying to get his brain into gear for any deep theological questions he might have to answer. "Fire away!"

"When are we 'aving the refreshments? Only my friend 'ere has gotta be goin' soon."

"I've got a question," said Stacy.

Here we go! I thought, she can't keep quiet, can she! She's just got to have an audience!

"How can God hear us all?" Stacy asked. "I mean, does God really hear me? I just feel so small! So insignificant!"

I was going to say, do you, then why do you always seem so self-obsessed? But Mum said, "Stacy! You're not insignificant. You're unique!" and I was going to say, "That's so true!" but didn't. Mum went on, "God really loves you, Stacy. He made you. He created you. He sent his Son to come and die for you and take the punishment for your sins so that nothing would get in the way of your friendship with him. He doesn't see our sin anymore; he sees Jesus in us. All the sin is gone - all that wrong stuff in us would separate us from our holy God - nailed to the cross with the Lord. We're his children, Stacy, when we ask Jesus to forgive us and take our sin away."

"Look at all the millions and billions and squillions of people on the planet," Stacy continued, as if she hadn't really heard what Mum had said, "have you ever watched all the people go by when you're waiting for a bus in Millstead town centre? All the people rushing by and not noticing you, getting on with lives you'll never know anything about! There are times when I feel really alone in the universe. Really

71

really alone. Do you know what I mean?"

"Yes," said a voice, unexpectedly. Kendra looked embarrassed to have spoken, but defiant. "Yes, I know what you mean. Everyone's so busy with their own lives. I don't think God really cares about us as individuals. I'm sorry, but I don't. Do you mind if I'm excused? I've got a terrible headache." And she disappeared upstairs, as one or two people glanced at each other and pulled faces, and my mum mumbled something about Kendra having had a difficult life, and Mr Skinner said we ought to pray for her. But they couldn't right then, because Mrs Kettle - apparently having had quite enough of spiritual things - stood up and said, "Tea, anyone?" and there was a general murmering of approval, except for Edna's friend who said she'd got to be going soon.

Mr Upson's hearing aid emitted an ear-shattering whistle at that point.

"Did the young lady want to know how God could hear us?"

"Yes," I muttered, "About an hour ago."

"God is Spirit," he said, his old watery eyes peering dimly at Stacy, "On a blustery day, you can't say where the wind is going or where it's been. You can see the evidence when you notice all the flowers little heads nodding here and there. It's like that with God, you know. Yes, it is. Unfathomable. Deep, very deep. Many questions we won't get the answers to till we're in Glory. But all we know is that he does hear us. He knows our words even before we've said 'em. Knows our hearts and minds. But he's God, you see. Almighty. And we aren't."

Stacy sat back in her seat and looked awestruck,

but then, she always looked a bit strange to me, so I took no notice: especially as the food came in then, and I proceeded to make a real pig of myself. But Mrs Kettle was just such a good cook.

Mum took a big plateful up to Kendra, and came down placing what I guessed was meant to be a comforting hand on my shoulder and saying Kendra was all right. I couldn't care less.

Then, Mum completely ruined the evening by announcing she and I would do the clearing away. Everyone else started leaving, except for Mr Skinner and Mr upson who had fallen asleep on the sofa... At least, I hoped it was sleep. He looked dead to me. Oh yeah and then there was Edna's friend who hadn't been going to stop long but seemed in no great hurry to move away from our TV.

In the end, I was left on my own to do acres and acres of washing up whilst Mum chatted with the minister who was worrying that no-one had got anything spiritual from the evening. I was just relieved that Stacy had gone and wasn't bothering me; she'd got a lift home with someone, which had prompted my mother to sigh loudly and say how inconvenient it was not to have a car. Considering it was absolutely ages since her old Ford had fallen apart and we managed perfectly well without it, I wasn't sure what she was making a fuss about. But then she'd said Alex was being a great help in sorting that out. "He's helping me get a new car, well, not a new one, just something that isn't 90 per cent rust," she'd smiled. That was all news to me and made me think about what Kendra had said earlier.

Without a doubt, Mum really was keen on Alex,

even though I didn't quite believe they were 'in love'. But I felt my heart start racing as I thought about Alex as a step-dad. I could imagine Mum and him curled up together totally ignoring me, planning a great new life together, even having a new baby!

"Oh, yuk!" I said.

Still, the fact was, my mum was thirty-five; an antique but not totally past it; a boy at school's mum had been older than her when she'd had twins. A new baby! Would I just be in the way, then? Would they wish it was just them and their new child or even children, kids who would take my mum's attention off me forever? And even if there weren't new kids, would she love Alex more than she loved me? Would she be so overwhelmed with him that I just didn't matter anymore? Would she turn into someone like my Aunty Ann, disappearing off with her man and leaving me on my own somewhere for an unknown amount of time? I realised I didn't know if Alex had been married or had had children; would there be step-kids to share my mum with? What had Kendra said - strangers who knew all her business?

"Oh God!" I groaned. "Oh God help!"

Wise Words and Rehearsals

There was a noise at the door, and I turned round, my hands deep in the suds, to see old Mr Upson standing unsteadily in the kitchen doorway.

"Are you all right, Mr U?"

"Oh yes, dear, quite all right. I think. I ate a bit much, you know. The old digestion..." His hearing aid whistled. "Was the video good? I didn't hear a lot of it. Still. Nice to see your friends. The other young people."

"Friends!" I snorted.

"Poor dears." He gripped the sink and steadied himself.

"Poor dears!" I exclaimed, "I'm not being horrible, Mr U," (I was) "but neither of them are poor. Just complete pains in the - neck."

He didn't seem to hear me. He took his glasses off and wiped his eyes and asked if there were any of Mrs Kettle's homemade shortbread biscuits left and when he found out there weren't he said, "Thank you Lord!" because he said the biscuits weren't good for him but sometimes he couldn't resist the temptation. Then I noticed my hands were horrid and red and wrinkly and snapped, "Where's my mother? Talking about Alex again I suppose! She was meant to help me!" And I clattered the plates very loudly as I began to dry them.

"Did you want me to help you do that, dear?"

I could just imagine my mum's face if the trembly

old man dropped her best china. Still, maybe it would serve her right for being so neglectful, not doing the plates herself. "No, better not, I suppose," I said, very ungraciously.

Mr Upson put his glasses back on. "Oysters. I heard that bit, dear, in the video. About the pearl of greatest price."

I was too busy fuming about my mum not helping with the washing up to comment.

"Ever tried 'em, dear?"

"Ever tried what?"

"Oysters. No? I love oysters. And prawns. D'you know how oysters get the pearl, dear?"

I liked Mr Upson. But right then I really wished he'd go away.

"They say it's a bit of sand gets into the poor old oyster and irritates it and somehow that's how the pearl gets made." He chuckled. "Amazing, isn't it?"

"Amazing," I said, not very enthusiastically.

"I've often found people are a bit like that sand sometimes, dear. Get into our lives and make us squirm. But somehow, these little irritations can bring about something of great worth in our life - if we let God handle it all."

I stopped clattering and looked at him. I knew Mr Upson often had incredible insight - as if God had given him some kind of gift to be able to know things maybe he didn't naturally know.

"Those girls," he said, nodding, "Macy and Dendro..."

I sighed, "Stacy and Kendra Mr U,"

"Uh-huh... that's right...Both deeply unhappy souls, you know."

"Unhappy! I'm the one who-"

"Don't think either of them know the Lord. Eh? Nope. At least you and me, we can share our problems with him. Those two are all alone. You pray for them, I hope?"

Pray for them! Not likely! I looked at him, exasperated, but he kept talking.

"The Lord Jesus wants us to love each other. 'Course, you know that, dear."

"Hah!" I remembered my mum telling me to show Stacy how much Jesus loved her, by being her friend. Mr Upson didn't seem to hear my exclamation. But then, he was terribly deaf.

"People are funny. They get on our nerves. They do things we don't like. They just aren't always what we want them to be. But then, neither is life. You can get all wound up and before you know it, you're all knotted up with anger towards folk and life. The more you think angry thoughts, the bigger they seem to get, until that's all you're feeling. You know, dear, anger and hate - and unforgiveness - blocks out the presence of God, just like clouds block out the sunshine."

He was right. I knew it. He was absolutely right.

"The Presence of God. Now, there's that pearl again. Get into the real presence of God and my word, you don't want to come out of it. It always knocks me out that we can enjoy his presence anywhere - even when we're doing the washing up! Peace, joy, glory. Wonderful. You never want to give in to anger or jealousy or unforgiveness or anything that'll stop you being in the presence of our dear Lord Jesus. How often we go out of that presence, even though we're his children!"

I leaned against the sink, my thoughts whirring about my brain. When I felt angry, everything else was blotted out. Mr Upson was right - it was like clouds gathering over the sun. I couldn't even pray when I was so uptight!

"Now dear, don't forget to pray for those young souls. I'll pray too. It's powerful stuff when two of you agree on something and come before the Lord with it. Now, you say those biscuits are all gone? Shame. But praise the Lord."

The next minute, he was all gone, too, because Mr Skinner took him home. Mum came into the kitchen and moaned that I hadn't done the dishes properly, and that she'd have to do them all over again. I told her it was her fault because she'd been so busy talking - I didn't say anything about Alex - and she told me I was being rude, which I was, and she didn't know why I was being so grumpy nowadays, and that Alex had said I seemed mature for my age, but she wasn't so sure. And I wanted to shout, "Who cares what Alex thinks!" but instead declared, almost as dramatically as Stacy might, "Sometimes I don't think you care what I feel about things at all!" and she told me to stop being silly and go to bed because I was getting over-tired and fractious. And I felt about six years old.

Next night, Wednesday, was a rehearsal night for the play. I was completely shattered by the time I struggled into the church hall. We'd had a maths test which Amanda and Stacy and everyone else had sailed through but which I'd thought was horrendously difficult; I don't know if I was just being incredibly thick but when I read a question about the hypotenuse

I thought about rhino-like creatures living in mud holes in Africa and after that I couldn't get my brain round anything in the test. Then Dinah had asked me to sort out something for her which I found utterly exhausting.

A girl in her class (and in the youth club) called Rowena Taylor who was a real snob and actually thought most people were 'common' had recently lost her granny. I don't mean she'd misplaced her - her granny, a Christian, had died. Rowena had told Dinah that her neighbour had said that the fact that the lights on the Taylor family Christmas tree were not working properly was down to Rowena's granny's ghost showing them she was still hanging around. Dinah had said, rubbish, when someone dies and knows Jesus they go straight to be with him and didn't hang around earth bothering people and playing with fairy lights. Rowena had replied she didn't know; her mum just said her dad was useless with electrics. Then she'd said, casually, that her neighbour had mentioned playing some sinister game with which she claimed she'd called up her Great Aunt Veronica. Dinah had been horrified and told Rowena, God said we mustn't try to contact the dead, and he loves us, so he must have said that for a good reason. Only she couldn't remember where he'd said it, so she asked me, and I didn't know either, so we spent lunch-time hunched over her Bible finding all the verses and showing them to Rowena.

Rowena had eventually seemed convinced, Dinah looked happy, and I felt so drained I nearly fell asleep in class that afternoon. Then I missed the bus home, had loads of homework, and what with ignoring mum and Kendra as much as I could - as I said before, by the time I showed up to the rehearsals, I was shattered. I was also late.

Alex, Tim and Stacy were on the stage, talking, and waving scripts around. The only other people there were Dinah and David, who were sitting almost on top of a radiator. I joined them. I felt relieved the little kids weren't there. I really couldn't have rustled up the energy to cope with them.

"It's freezing," I observed, dolefully.

"Hello, Sammy." Dinah's eyes were fixed on the stage. I opened a can of Fizzy juice as Tim and Alex went off stage.

"Stacy's a good actress," whispered Dinah.

"Yeah, right," I said, wearily, remembering I'd left my chewing gum at home, "Did she tell you that? Sounds like our Stacy all right."

"No, I've been watching - you'll see."

They were rehearsing where Stacy - the time traveller, or TT in the script, which I immediately recognised as standing for Toothy Twit - finds herself in the present day. I felt very sceptical as I began to watch. After hearing so much about Stacy's own high opinions of her acting, I really did expect her to be a dreadful actress, probably totally over the top and laughable.

"Oh!" she said, rolling her eyes in the most dramatic fashion, "Where am I?"

I thought, Ivy Street church hall, you dope, but then Tim walked on stage, and I sighed, longingly. He looked fantastic, in black jeans and sweatshirt. "Hey there!" called Stacy, loudly, "Can you tell me the date?"

I couldn't hear Tim's answer so well - he

mumbled a little - but I caught, "Christmas eve," and Stacy's silly pop eyes almost fell out of their sockets. "I have to tell you my story! You will never believe where I've been, what I've seen! Will you give me a minute of your time?"

Don't, I thought, cruelly, you'll regret it - you'll never get rid of her.

"Yes," said Tim, "If you'll let me tell you my story, too."

"I've been to a place far away. I've seen a baby born, who - whom - they said was the Saviour of the world!" Stacy flung her arms out and nearly managed to sock Tim in the jaw, "I saw that baby grown up, and killed, I've seen his mother weep!"

Tim tried to look surprised but didn't do it very well. "I don't believe it!"

"It's true!" Stacy nodded so violently I thought she'd crick her neck.

"But in a way, that's my story, too - I believe in a baby who was born over two thousand years ago," Tim glanced down at his script and I couldn't hear what he was saying for a moment. Then he looked up again and said, "...Saviour of the world, who grew up and showed us what God is like, who healed the sick and set people free - who died on the cross for my sin and yours!"

"I've seen him!" said Stacy, and for a moment I thought she really had, she seemed so excited.

"I've met him!" stated Tim, very stiffly.

"How can this be?" Stacy put a hand up to her mouth in mock wonderment, "You're not a time traveller too, are you?"

"Anyone can meet him today! You've just got to

ask him into your heart!"

"Stop!" said Alex, who was standing by the door. He went up to the stage. "Tim, this is probably the most important part of the play. You're telling people how to come to know Jesus! I can hardly hear you at the back of the hall. I can hear Stacy, no trouble." Alex turned to us. "Could you hear everything, over there?"

"I couldn't hear my brother as well as I could hear Stacy," said Dinah.

"I'm sorry," Tim shrugged, "I'm just not a natural actor like Stacy is."

I nearly choked on my energy drink.

"Oh Tim, you're just fine," smiled Stacy, sweetly, "He's very good really, isn't he, Alex!"

"Yes, he is, Stacy, but he needs to project his voice. Tim! Speak up, loudly, slowly."

They ran through the scene one more time. Tim was louder, but he didn't sound very natural. Stacy, on the other hand, seemed to truly believe she actually was the traveller who had seen Jesus born and crucified in ancient Palestine. As I kept watching, she almost made me believe it too. In fact, I realised, and I hated to admit it, Stacy was - surprisingly - a good actress, even if she did have a tendency to be melodramatic. Grudgingly, I saw she breathed life into the play, life that hadn't been there when I'd read through her part with Tim before.

"Told you she was good!" Dinah murmured to me. I said nothing.

David and Dinah and I wandered over to the stage. Alex enthused and encouraged and Tim asked who was going to be in charge of flashing the lights on and off when Stacy was 'time-travelling', because did we know that David had been involved with that sort of thing in a school play last term? David went red and muttered something about having only helped and not being very good at it. Alex laughed and put his arm round David's shoulder.

A picture flashed into my mind of his arm round my mum. I suddenly felt very icy towards Alex, and when he offered me a lift home I said "No thanks," so sharply he looked taken aback. However, I quickly regretted it, because Tim asked Alex if he could could give him and Dinah a lift, then, Stacy said she'd "adore a lift, if you can squeeze little me in!" And when Alex said yes, Stacy said, goofily, "God bless you!" I would've laughed at her if I hadn't been so gutted at missing my chance of sitting with Tim in the back of Alex's car. I stood there sulking a bit wishing thatStacy would stop trying to sound pious and devout in front of Tim - it made me hopping mad - especially since I didn't think she was a real Christian at all, and, I remembered, neither did Mr Upson. And he was the sort of person who'd know those kind of things.

"Perhaps we can practice somewhere together, Tim," said Stacy, "I'm sure I can help you project your voice and all that." Instead of looking revolted, Tim actually said, "Thanks, Stacy, that's nice of you!" and Stacy said, smugly, "We'll talk about it on the way home!"

"I'll be a bit late for the next rehearsal on Saturday," Alex announced as he put on his coat, "So you'll be in charge for a little while, Sam, OK?"

I glanced at him, coldly. "OK. Tim! We can practice your voice projection then. I don't think you'll need any extra lessons from Stacy." Tim didn't look quite so relieved as I'd hoped he'd look.

"I'm not happy about you walking home in the dark on your own," Alex said to me.

"You sound like my mum!" I told him, rudely. I would like to have added, and you're not, and you're not my dad, either, but I didn't have the nerve.

"Sam!" Tim was beckoning to me. It occurred to me that was the first time he'd actually spoken to or even acknowledged me that evening. But it didn't matter - his face was full of concern as he said, quietly, "Sam, you don't have to walk home alone, you know."

My heart skipped a beat. Was he going to offer to forgo his lift and walk me home himself? How romantic! I felt like sticking my tongue out at Stacy in childish triumph.

Tim kept talking. "Well, you're a friend, Sam. A mate! And I look out for my friends. You know, I bet David'll walk with you!" He winked at me. "I think he fancies you."

"What!"

"Hey! Stace, why don't you come to Parkside youth club? You could come along with Sam," Tim said, as if he'd thought of something wonderful, "You'd have a great laugh, wouldn't she, Sam?"

Frost sparkled on the pavements and stars glittered overhead as I walked home that night. People who had old chimneys in their houses had lit their fires, and smoke wisped into the sky. Alex's car shot past with Tim and Stacy crammed together in the back. David trudged off alone up South Street. And the world was cold.

I arrived home only to find my mum excitedly

planning a Christmas shopping trip; even Kendra looked more alive than usual, and almost interested.

"Where shall we go? Ipswich, Colchester, or Bury St Edmunds? None are too far by train," said Mum, "There's not much selection in Millstead, is there?"

I'd always found Millstead perfectly adequate for shopping - it had a music store called 'Sounds' and that was all I cared about. Not that I cared much about anything right then. All I was was Tim's 'friend'. I didn't know a great deal about boys but I knew enough to realise when Tim called me a friend and suggested I walk home with David. It meant that he didn't fancy me. I was so disappointed I could cry. So I searched in the bread bin for a packet of crisps to help ease some of my misery, and decided to go upstairs and just sprawl on my bed and feel miserable.

"You'll have a great time!" Mum said, "Sam! Are you listening? We'll go on Saturday!"

"What? I can't. Rehearsals."

"Oh, never mind rehearsals for once! It's a special trip! I'll have a word with Al - "

"We don't usually go on a special Christmas shopping trip - you can get a mouldy old turkey and a few sad crackers in the supermarket on South Street."

"Samantha! You've never had a sad cracker in your life! What a thing to say!" Mum looked genuinely upset and somewhere deep inside - simmering below all the anger and unhappiness - I felt bad about that. After all, we'd never had much money, but she'd always made Christmas really nice for me. "Anyhow, Sam, I'm earning more this year, with this new job, so I'd like to celebrate a bit and get some lovely gifts this year. That's all! I thought you'd be pleased!"

I wasn't pleased about anything. Tim didn't fancy me.

"And anyway, usually it's just the two of us, but we aren't sure who's going to be around this Christmas, so we ought to make a good effort. We might have Kendra, and Aunty Ann and Bo, and we might even have Alex !"

Aagh! What a threat!

"You go. I'm not interested," I said, "I'm going upstairs."

"With that large packet of fattening crisps?" asked Kendra.

"Oh shut up, stick face!" I said. Then Mum had hauled me aside and told me firmly that I'd better buck my ideas up because I may not like Kendra, but she was my cousin, and I seemed to have taken a Backward Step in my Christian Life and she was very disappointed in me.

Disappointed!

I wanted to yell, all right, I didn't like Kendra, but that wasn't all that was wrong - life stank at present, and frankly I was disappointed with everything, because Tim didn't fancy me! I was fed up with her too, with her constant Alex this and Alex that and Alex always turning up on our doorstep and Alex giving us lifts and Alex telling her what car to buy and Alex probably coming for Christmas! But I didn't have the guts so I just glared instead. Mum said I was getting to be really unlikeable just lately and she hoped it wasn't a horrid teenage phase I wasn't going to come out of until I was twenty. And I tried to look hard and cool but I wasn't hard and I didn't feel at all cool.

Out of my Life

I don't know why, but whenever I get upset about anything, I always wake up at ten past three in the morning.

This time, it was as if a huge pit of misery had just welled up and engulfed me in the silence of my sleep. Images swirled about in the fretful blackness. Tim, who thought I was a 'friend'! Kendra talking about step-dads. And my mum smiling that big-eyed pathetic smile at Alex that said 'my hero!'. It turned my stomach the way she simpered up at him.

Would she marry Alex? What a thought. I imagined her in a white frothy dress looking like some ancient meringue. Would I have to be the bridesmaid? What a revolting idea. I could almost see the sparkly ring on Mum's third finger, left hand. I caught my breath. There was already a ring on that finger, a ring she had never taken off, the ring my dad had put there years ago.

I didn't often think about my dad. There wasn't much point because I could barely remember him. All I could really recall was a tall dark haired man smiling when a very small me had offered him a big bunch of daisies. As much as I racked my brains I couldn't remember anything else of him; I could see in my mind some of the photos of him in our album - on holiday, holding me as a baby - a fat cherub with big ears. There were a few of him digging the garden wearing a funny straw hat; then there was the one that

Mum didn't like to look at, the one of him leaning proudly on the bonnet of the blue car - the one he'd had the accident in.

Hot tears began to run down my cheeks. I couldn't fathom why. It had all happened so long ago now. Mum had said we shouldn't cry for Dad, he was with Jesus, and when we went to be with Jesus, we'd see Dad again. If I ever felt sad about not having a dad at home, Mum said that I should remember that. And when I was very young that's just what I did. Then life seemed to move on and somehow I suppose in a way the world turned and we left Dad behind.

But right then, that chill winter night, I realised how very much I missed him. And that I'd always miss him, forever. Oh, I felt so lonely, as if I had nothing, was nothing. Even the boy I liked didn't fancy me. Maybe Kendra was right - my looks must be absolutely foul, as she was always so slyly assuring me. Then, unexpectedly, an image flashed into my mind. Mr Upson - I could almost see his kind, smiley eyes. His words were coming back to me.

"Those girls...don't think either of them know the Lord. Eh? Nope. At least you and me, we can share our problems with him. Those two are all alone. You pray for them, I hope?"

I didn't feel as if I had the Lord at all right then. I was the one who was alone.

"Jesus!" I whispered in the darkness. "Jesus!"

I bit my lip and wiped my eyes with the back of my hand. What on earth had happened to me? I'd been so irritable lately! Always fuming! Where had that lovely presence of God gone? I recalled what Mr Upson had said about anger and negative stuff like that blocking God's presence.

"But it's not my fault life stinks and that those - those - people make me mad!"

I still didn't feel his presence.

I tried desperately to remember the other things Mr Upson had said - had he said how to find God's presence again after you seemed to have lost it? I felt confused.

"Oh Jesus, please help me!"

Then a thought came into my muddled mind and I switched on my bedside lamp and rummaged about on the little shelf where I kept tissues and books and my emergency biscuits in case I was hungry in the night. I found my Bible, and I'm ashamed to admit, it had a lot of dust on the cover.

I didn't know where to look for help, so I just let the Bible fall open. And I saw these words: 'Cast all your anxiety upon him because he cares for you' (1 Peter 5:7). I breathed in sharply. It was almost like God speaking directly to me - an invitation to share my burden with him. In that instant, I didn't feel alone anymore, and it was such a relief.

"Jesus! You are still here! You do care about me!"

Tears fell down onto my sheet as I told him all my problems. They all came tumbling out in no specific order: all the stuff about Tim not fancying me, and how horrible Kendra was, and the total irritation I'd felt with Stacy, and how worried I was about Mum and Alex. Nothing happened when I'd finished; God didn't send a big angel to tell me everything would be OK. I just knew he'd heard, that was all. I knew I had to really trust him that he would handle everything...my mum was always saying, 'And we know that in all things God works for the good of those who love him, who have been called according to his purpose' (Romans 8:28). At that moment, that Scripture really seemed to mean something to me. In fact, I felt quite excited - maybe God would make Tim fancy me after all! And make Mum and Alex fall out. And make Kendra go home. Tomorrow!

"Lord, I'll try not to get angry anymore! I'll really try!" I said. I suddenly had a feeling God wanted me to pray for Stacy and Kendra as Mr Upson had suggested. But no. I just couldn't promise to do that! After all, it was their fault I'd been angry! Exhausted, I dozed off - and woke up the next morning late for school because I'd slept through my alarm clock's shrieking.

"Wake up!" Mum was pummelling me and Kendra was standing there in the doorway, toothbrush in one hand, smirking and saying, "Fancy having to have your mummy wake you up at your age!" Then I realised I had a sore throat, which meant I didn't feel like eating any breakfast and Mum insisted I went to the doctor that morning. And what with all the hassle, I forgot that I'd prayed in the night - until I was sitting in the doctor's surgery surrounded by sick and coughing old folk and felt the need to pray for protection from any germs that might be zapping about. Which was a bit of cheek really, considering I was a walking germ myself. I remembered God might make Tim fancy me at any minute, and I began to feel quite happy. Until Dr Summers - who always seemed to be totally cheerful even if you were practically dying - brightly told me I had a virus that was going round and I realised, with a stab of annoyance, I'd caught it from Stacy. Then the doctor told me I'd be better off staying home for a few days and my happy feelings disappeared completely when I thought of spending time in the house alone with my cousin.

I trudged home and told her I had a virus and she said "Coo, how disgusting," and avoided me afterwards, so at least we didn't get into any arguments and she didn't get close enough to make any sarky remarks. I lolled about in my room and felt ill for a while, and then realised I really couldn't go on the dreary shopping trip which they'd decided was going to be to Bury St Edmunds, so that was a bonus. In fact, the twinkling ray of hope I'd felt when I'd told God my problems got stronger; until I had a phone call on the Friday evening from Amanda.

"You haven't missed much at school! Old Sims asked me if I was day-dreaming in maths and I said no, I was actually thinking about how I could save the life of a millionaire and get rewarded with pots of money. Then I had to spend the rest of the boring lesson calculating the odds of that happening, which were pretty slim, I can tell you. Oh, and here's something else with slim odds. You'll never guess. It's too unreal. Stacy has got - wait for it! - a boyfriend."

"A boyfriend?" My throat felt dry - and it wasn't just the virus.

"Yeah, would you believe it? Some guy she met who goes to the grammar school. He phoned her up and invited her to a disco at his school. I can't believe anyone with half a brain would want Stacy. Amazing, isn't it? I wonder what's wrong with him?" Amanda cackled down the line, "I mean, what wimp would want to go out with that freak? I bet he's weird - must be, to fancy Stacy!"

I couldn't speak. It wasn't possible...was it? No...surely not! Tim couldn't possibly...he wouldn't...he could never fancy that unattractive, totally unspeakable Stacy! My worst fears were realised when she continued.

"Now all she can talk about is 'Tim' this and 'Tim' that," Amanda was sniggering, "Makes a change from boring us to tears with her acting ambitions I suppose! Honestly! Stacy Morgan! Yuk! I wish I could meet this boy, just get a look at him! What a dope he must be, really!"

My voice was hoarse. "You have met him, Amanda. It's Tim. My Tim!"

"What?" Silence. "Oh, you're kidding, never! Not your Tim! I never thought - I didn't for one moment think it was the same boy - Sammy! How on earth did that happen?"

"I'm - I'm not sure!"

"Well, there's got to be something wrong with him if he really does fancy her. I thought so, didn't I, when I met him? I cannot believe this. She's awful!"

"Yes, I know, Amanda." I gulped back my tears. I didn't want Kendra coming into the hallway and catching me crying on the phone! "Can we change the subject?"

"I mean, look at her. The complete hag, pinching your boy! She's not even pretty! What does he see in her? Are you going to confront her when you're back? I'd kill her. Yes, I would. Truly. Pretends to be your friend, greases up to you - then whack! Gets your boy from under your nose! And she is so incredibly plain! I cannot believe it!"

I put the phone down and felt my self esteem crawl out of the door. I felt ugly and small and demoralised. I also felt spotty and fat and if Kendra knew she would have said, "Told you so."

Almost as soon as I'd replaced the receiver, the phone rang again. It was Alex.

"Hello!" His voice was so buoyant it grated on my nerves. "Hi, Sams. How y'doing? Can I have a word with your mum?"

I swallowed down the last of my tears. Oh! There was my Tim going off with some horrendous girl with no fashion sense and disgusting teeth and hair - and what did it say about me that he preferred that? Now here was this interfering man, Alex, after my mum again! How unfair life was! I should be the one with the love life, not my mum!

"Alex," I said, choking a bit on my words, "I've got something to tell you."

"Oh yes? What's that, then?"

"I'm not going to be at the rehearsals tomorrow."

"Ah - yes, your mum said you might be going shopping. It's OK, love."

Love! What a nerve! I wasn't his love! I wasn't anyone's love!

"No, I'm ill, so I can't go anyway."

"Yes, I know you're not well, your mum told me."

What had Kendra said about strangers knowing all your business? This man - this person I hadn't even known a few months ago - knew I was ill! Maybe it was because I was feeling grotty, but that struck me as appalling. How dare my mum tell Alex my business! I forgot she worked with him - and probably all her office knew I was poorly, too, and it didn't really matter. Right then, Alex knowing my intimate business really bothered me.

"No, look, Alex, I shan't be coming to help with the play anymore. Ever. I'm just too busy."

"What?"

"I've got this massive project on Hawaii to finish. I'm behind with it. Pretty stuck actually. There's only so much you can write about pineapples and hula dancers. So I've got to really work hard on it. I can't be involved with the play anymore."

"Sam, I'm really sorry - the kids will be so upset! They love you!"

I felt a lump in my throat. Then I thought, Tim won't be upset.

"I'll get my mum." But Mum was already in the hallway - I felt anger creep up my body, and contempt, too, as I realised she must've been expecting a call from Alex, and was rushing to speak to her darling as if she were a teenager! Ugh, yuk, yuk, yuk!

"What did I hear you say then? You're not going to be involved in the play?"

"That's right." I handed the phone to her, "It's Alex," I said, deliberately.

"But you loved being involved - with all your friends!"

Precisely, I thought, all my friends! I just couldn't bear the thought of seeing Stacy and Tim together - no, no, no! And even as my mum started talking to Alex, and telling me he was very sad that I wasn't going to be involved, I felt a quick spark of pleasure - I'd caused that man some grief. Mum didn't say anything when she came back into the room, but she eyed me as if she wanted to say something but didn't like to. I was glad she didn't make any remarks - I wasn't in the mood. Life was terrible.

"God, how could you let this happen? I told you my problems, I felt you'd heard, I hoped you'd work it out for my good! I thought you'd make Tim fancy me - not fancy Stacy! Everything's just got worse!"

The very thought of that toothy rat in her thin white cardigan winning the heart of my lovely Timothy Aldridge Watson made me feel even sicker than I already did. Pray for her? Never! And sullenly, I thought, Mum and Alex still seem friendly, too, and Kendra hasn't gone home! Huh! So much for God handling things! I said I was too ill to go to church that Sunday. I wasn't, I just didn't feel like going.

Back at school on Monday, the first thing that happened was I was almost mown down in a corridor by Dinah who was wide-eyed because she'd just found out I wasn't going to be involved with the play anymore.

"I'm too busy!" I said. But I did feel bad about letting Dinah and the little kids down. That was Stacy's fault, though, wasn't it! Amanda told me straight away, I should 'confront' Stacy, or even get Trina Finch to do it for me. And I knew immediately 'confront' meant 'bash'.

"But I suppose you'll say Jesus never thumped anyone, so you won't!" Amanda rolled her eyes. She didn't see me clench my fists as I thought: "I'd love to thump her!"

Still, I knew in my heart it would serve no purpose to confront Stacy. It wouldn't make Tim like me, would it? And it might even make Stacy smug to think she'd got someone I wanted. So I resolved I'd just never speak to her or look at her ever again. Amanda said she couldn't be a Christian in a thousand years if you couldn't sort people out who'd hurt you. She actually thought I was being saintly. But she didn't see my heart.

Anyway, I did what I said. I didn't speak or look at Stacy. She tried to be her usual obnoxious friendly self, desperate to talk about 'my new boyfriend, Tim!' It was obvious that she was eye-poppingly thrilled (and probably a little stunned, as I was) that a good-looking boy had asked her out. She was telling anyone who'd sit still long enough that 'he's gorgeous, Sammy'll tell you, she knows him!' Oh! I tried to play it very cool as if I didn't care. Trouble was, I couldn't keep my cool forever.

The following Friday, Amanda was off sick with the throat virus. I'd had yet another encounter with Dinah that morning - she had informed me that her brother's new girlfriend, Stacy, was going to Parkside youth club, which of course meant I couldn't go: well, it didn't really, and yet, it did. At any rate, I really felt Stacy Morgan had ruined my life, so she was the last person I wanted to see as I stalked into the loos at lunch-time.

No-one else was there but me and her.

She was washing her hands and when she saw me in the mirror, she seemed a bit startled. I began feeling a very familiar anger. She looked even more ridiculous than usual. She'd been practising for her part in 'The Christmas Heist' production for the Winter Gala which was only a week or so away. She had been trying her costume on and was dressed as a Christmas tree, all in green, with baubles hanging, and a star on her head.

This was the girl Tim preferred to me. I just could not understand how he fancied Stacy. Amanda, yes. Even Kendra. But not Stacy!

"Hello, Sammy!"

She sounded a little nervous.

"I - er - I haven't seen much of you lately. We've both been very busy, haven't we? Me with all the rehearsals for 'The Christmas Heist' and 'Lord of Time' and my boyfriend. You - well, with your project on Hawaii, someone said. Are you too busy to come to Parkside tonight? We'll all be there. Me and Tim and David. We'd love to see you!"

I moved to the washbasins.

"Er - I notice you've been a bit distracted. All that work on the project I expect. Sammy? Are you OK? Maybe you should try to chill out a bit. Do come tonight."

I ran the hot tap. She looked anxious. "We're still friends - aren't we?" I didn't answer. I wiped my hands on a paper towel.

"Um - I haven't done anything to offend you, have I?"

"You breathe," I muttered, "That's enough."

"Sammy! I thought there was something wrong between us. I just don't know why you're like this with me. It's preposterous. You sound quite aggressive."

"Aggressive!" I was going to say, Amanda suggested I thumped you. That's aggressive! But I didn't, because she was bleating away like a silly sheep.

"I've just got this feeling you don't like me anymore. And that's terrible, because we're both Christians. I've been lying awake at night, losing sleep, tossing and turning - " her voice rang out dramatically, "Your face has been before me, this tragic - "

"Save it for the stage," I said.

"Tragic face! And all I could think was - maybe poor old Sammy liked my boyfriend, Tim, and was a bit upset with me, because Tim and I are an item?"

Oh! Surely she hadn't snared him purely to spite me, to get some kind of weird satisfaction out of pinching a boy I fancied? Whatever, I was absolutely not going to help boost her self esteem by admitting she'd won him when I wanted him! I'd never admit it! Never, never, never!

"Stacy, you really are stupid! I didn't like Tim - well, not like that. He's a friend!" and my heart lurched as I said that word. "If you must know, I've just had enough of you. You get on my nerves."

"Oh!"

I sneered at her with a sneer worthy of my cousin. "I just don't want to be around you anymore. I never did. I only made friends with you because my mum said I should." She seemed shocked, and I felt gratified. "You may as well know - I never liked you. I only pretended. Actually, nobody likes you. We all hate you."

"Sammy! I can't - I can't believe - "

I leaned towards her, threateningly. She backed away, baubles jiggling. "Stacy, just shut up! And keep out of my way. Or else. OK?"

I stalked out of the cloakroom, feeling big and powerful. Both Christians! Liar! As if she was a Christian! What a weasel that girl is! I thought.

It didn't take long for the powerful feelings to subside and then I realised that being unpleasant to

Stacy in the loos, whilst momentarily satisfying, hadn't actually made me feel any better about life. But at least Stacy kept out of my way from then on.

Yes, at last, she was out of my life. Until the night of the Winter Gala.

This New Life

"Coo," said Kendra, "There's a really funny smell in this school isn't there?"

"It isn't the school, it's you."

"Or you. It's all that chewing. I wonder why your mum hasn't asked Alex to come."

"Why should she? He isn't my parent. Look about you. The hall's packed with parents. It's a parent's evening. OK?"

"I'm not your parent. I'm here. I wonder if your mum and Alex are OK? He hasn't been around that much lately, has he?"

I shook my head, gloomily. "He's been on a couple of business trips. Then there's been the rehearsals for the Lord of Time."

"Oh, so the step-dad is still in the picture."

"Shut up!"

She scratched her elegant bare leg. "Coo, this is going to be boring."

I was inclined to agree with her: 'The Christmas Heist' wasn't likely to be so much fun as last year's Gala offering. Five boys from Year 11 had formed their own band and sang some songs (with very rude lyrics), which resulted in them being thrown off the stage by the caretaker and the head of the English department. Still, I wasn't going to let Kendra know I agreed, so I said, "You think everything's boring."

"That shopping trip to Bury St Edmunds with your mum wasn't. It was great."

Hmm, I thought, yes - she and mum had gone together and they both seemed to have really enjoyed it, coming back exhausted but jolly, laden down with interesting packages, some of which were whisked upstairs and hidden in the wardrobe, which I thought was excellent, as they were obviously meant for me. Mum had produced a very flashy tie she'd bought for Alex. I said it was putrid. Kendra had shown me some perfume she'd bought my mum, and she'd looked really happy. It had struck me I hadn't actually ever seen her look so genuinely happy before. Or at least, for years and years.

An enormous family row erupted in the seats in front of us just then - it was Trina Finch and her family, and they seemed to be arguing about where they were going on holiday, which I found very odd because there were still nineteen days to go till Christmas (I knew - I was counting). Then Mrs Finch said, "Well, I'm not going to that hotel in the Mendips again!" and I wondered where the Mendips were. I couldn't even remember the last time we'd had a holiday, Mum and me, so I didn't suppose we'd be going anywhere next summer.

"Look out," said Kendra, "It's starting. Yawn, yawn."

Some of the kids who played for the school orchestra started up a reedy sounding fanfare, the lights dimmed, parents stopped nattering, and kids calmed down. The curtain went up.

Stacy, two kids dressed like parcels and one poor child who had a turkey costume on were standing there looking idiotic. They said a few lines between them, then the scene changed and Stacy, the presents and the turkey were gone, and the fantasy musical swung into action. And I only had a moment to think about how totally silly that little worm had looked - the worm who got my boy - the worm I'd made friends with against my wishes - when the musical started getting really exciting and I got caught up in it; so did Kendra, she was stamping her feet and applauding with the rest of us, and seemed to forget to pose and look sophisticated. But the whole play was really good and very noisy and the girl who was playing the lead role was a great singer. She was also Trina Finch's sister, and Trina's dad started taking what seemed to be thousands of reels of film, snap, snap snapping away, standing up, crouching, bobbing around right in front of me, and completely obscuring my view. So I whispered to Mum that I was going to stand at the back. She nodded, and I got up and went to the back of the hall.

Two people were standing by the exit sign. One was Miss Grieves, the drama teacher. She had her arm round a kid who appeared to be quietly crying into a dangling mass of soggy loo paper.

I glanced at the kid. It was Stacy! She wasn't in her silly costume anymore.

"What's happened?" I said.

"Her mum and dad didn't turn up!" Miss Grieves whispered.

"It doesn't matter," said Stacy, but it clearly did. She was wiping her eyes and making a huge effort to stop crying. Miss Grieves smiled at her, warmly, then she looked at me. "Sammy! Stacy's one of your friends, isn't she? Maybe she can come and sit with you and your family for the rest of the Gala?"

Stacy blew her nose. She seemed flattened, deflated, smaller; totally different from her usual bumptious self. Was she putting it on to get sympathy? Her nose was huge, red and swollen, and her eyes were like little slits.

I shook my head. "Sorry. There's no room near me."

I crept back to my seat, my eyes resting only momentarily on the spare seat next to my cousin. And a smile appeared on my face in the darkness. Ha, ha ha! I thought. Serves the little witch right! Hers were the only parents in the entire school not to come. I'm glad! My heart filled with a feeling of real victory. I pushed down any thoughts that my elated feelings weren't very nice at all and certainly not very loving - why should I love Stacy? Mr Upson's words came unwelcomingly into my mind: Jesus wants us to love people! But I cast those thoughts aside. Ha, ha ha! Stacy's suffering! Good.

I was feeling pretty pleased with myself as we walked home. It had started to snow - I like snow - and Mum and Kendra were giggling as they held on to each other, trying to keep their feet. All I could think of was how glad I was that Stacy had been hurt. And my heart suddenly leapt. God had seen my anguish after all! He had heard me when I'd poured out my troubles that night! I remembered thinking I must trust him to work everything out for good. It had taken over two weeks, but at last, he was starting to sort it out, bringing me happiness, making Stacy miserable!

"Hooray! Thank you God!" Then I felt unexpectedly awful. Something was wrong. But what?

Maybe God wasn't happy with me because I hadn't prayed much lately. To be honest, I'd been so upset - and yes, cross - with God for letting Stacy and Tim go out together I hadn't actually prayed for over a fortnight. I said a quick "sorry!" but I still didn't feel the warm glow of his presence. Oh dear. What had happened to my walk with Jesus? Something was wrong, very wrong.

I shoved some gum in my mouth, feeling self-righteous. None of anything that had happened lately was my fault. It was Stacy's. And Tim's. And Kendra's. And Mum's and Alex's. And now - ha ha! Stacy was suffering - then I had a weird feeling God wasn't pleased with me for being glad about that. I felt cold, and it wasn't because of the snow. I somehow just knew Stacy being miserable wasn't part of God's plan for good at all.

"Stacy made a good Christmas tree," said Mum, "I didn't see her parents. It's a shame they stopped coming to the church. I wonder if they go to Parkside? Alex says Stacy's going to Parkside now with her friends..."

Friends! My boy, she meant! God, I thought, you know she deserves to suffer!

"Alex didn't say her parents were going...I must ask him."

I scuffed through the thin layer of fluffy snowflakes which had started to cover the pavement. Could my mum actually have a conversation without using the word 'Alex'? I wished he'd go away on business permanently, and stay away. Something told me deep in my heart that my mum was much happier than she had been in ages now she had Alex in her life. But I didn't care. I wanted him gone. Anywhere. Anyhow. Just gone.

It snowed like mad all that Saturday night, great swirling flakes covering the town in a big white blanket. My nice thoughts of triumph over Stacy had been completely flattened by the growing and growing and GROWING sense of God not being happy with me. I didn't know what to do about that, so tried to push it to the back of my mind by shoving my head under the pillow when it was time to get up. Somehow, I just knew I'd feel even more uncomfortable if I had to go to church. But Mum had fried bacon and eggs for breakfast and the smell of bacon tempted me downstairs.

"I don't know if I feel up to church this morning," I muttered, "Not feeling so brilliant."

Kendra tittered and I noticed she had a small amount of bacon on her plate.

"I thought you were a vegetarian?" I said.

"Aunty Katy," she said, loudly, "I think Sam wants to stay home and build a snowman."

"I do not!"

"The way you're wolfing down that bacon and egg breakfast I don't think there's much wrong with you, Samantha!" my mum observed, dryly. "Of course you'll come to church this morning. Kendra's coming, too. She wants to come. Don't you, Kendra?"

"Does she?" I couldn't help but snort. "She hasn't wanted to come before!"

"I want a chance to chuck a snowball at you!" Kendra's make-up mask cracked into a small smile as my mum winked at her. And she didn't chuck a snowball at me as we walked to church through several inches of snow, watching cross people trying to clear their paths with shovels. A couple of boys were building a snowman and Kendra asked if I wanted to go and help the kiddies in their fun. I said get lost. I cruelly imagined Stacy being hit in the face by a snowball thrown by me and wished it could come true.

There weren't many folk at the morning service, due to the snow, I guessed. Mr Upson wasn't there. One of the other people who hadn't turned up was the woman who took Bible Class so I had to stay in the church for the sermon - which meant I kept my seat by the warm radiator. Mr Skinner started to read a psalm. I didn't take a lot of notice. I was still wondering how I could get to snowball Stacy, and maliciously hoping she hadn't managed to reduce the size of her swollen red nose before she saw Tim at Parkside Fellowship that morning. How could she even pretend she was a Christian!

'O Lord, you have searched me and you know me. You know when I sit and when I rise; you perceive my thoughts from afar. You discern my going out and my lying down; you are familiar with all my ways. Before a word is on my tongue, you know it completely, O Lord.'

Mr Skinner looked up from his Bible.

"How special we are to God! He knows us so intimately! He cares! He even knows our thoughts! He knows what troubles us, what makes us happy, what upsets us!"

It would make me really happy to chuck a snowball at Stacy, I thought.

"Yes, God knows the heart," Mr Skinner went on, "People look at the outside...they see someone who is beautiful or handsome, but they don't see what's going on inside. God does."

I half shut my eyes wishing the service was over.

"Yes, he sees the inside, he sees if someone loves and cares, or does an act of kindness. He sees if people hate, too, even secretly, or wish ill on others - others that maybe have hurt us."

Oh! Was he talking to me?

"What's the matter?" hissed Kendra. "Stop squirming! Have you got fleas?"

"You know," said Mr Skinner, "there's that line in the Lord's prayer: 'Forgive us our debts, as we also have forgiven our debtors'. You see, Jesus said if we want to be forgiven, we have to forgive others. I think it's hard to forgive, especially when we may feel we're the victim in a situation. But still Jesus says we must forgive. I think it's a bit easier to do that if we remember how much he's forgiven each one of us."

I realised now - Mr Skinner wasn't actually talking to me. God was! It had hit me suddenly, like a freight train. He knows my thoughts! He knows my heart! He knows how HORRIBLE I am! He wasn't pleased with my thoughts at all! I knew he wasn't pleased with a lot of the things I'd been saying, either. I felt panic stricken. That was why God wasn't happy with me! That was why I couldn't feel his wonderful warm presence. He really didn't like my nasty thoughts, especially my feelings of hate towards Stacy, my gloating over her misery! But she'd hurt me! She deserved to suffer! It wasn't my fault that people were making my life difficult! I deserved all the sympathy! Didn't I?

"God, you must be joking. No way can I forgive

Stacy. I'm not going to let her off the hook. She's horrible. She pinched my boy and she's been a pain in the backside ever since I met her. And Kendra, too - I wish she'd just go away, and Alex!"

"- and if we aren't willing to forgive, we grieve the Holy Spirit. Yes, bad thoughts and deeds do grieve him. It's the Spirit who reveals Jesus to our hearts. The Spirit makes the Lord real to us! He makes real his presence. It makes him sad when we don't love others, and we don't feel the warmth of his fellowship when we harbour resentment and anger and unforgiveness."

"Oh! I've made the Spirit of God sad!" I remembered Mr Upson's words about anger blotting out the sunshine of God's presence. I didn't want to forgive! But right then I wanted with all my heart to be forgiven - and know his forgiveness and kindness and peace again! But how? How could I do it? I really loathed Stacy - and my cousin - and I was still cross in my heart with Alex - and my mum - and I was cross with Tim, too! And yes, I was even cross with God!

"Samantha! Could you be a dear, collect the hymn books and put them in the back room?"

The service was over. People were filing out. My mum was talking to old Edna and her friend and Kendra was browsing the book shelf at the back of the church. Mr Skinner was smiling at me. I had to tell someone. I just had to.

"Mr Skinner, I've got a massive problem."

"Well, dear, I know you've been busy lately. Is it this project on Hawaii? I hope you know you can always talk to me about anything that's troubling you."

"What? Hawaii? No! Mr Skinner, I'm angry."

"Oh? Anger isn't always wrong, you know, Samantha. Jesus got angry. There's such a thing as 'righteous anger'. We can feel angry on behalf of someone else because they're being mis-treated, for instance."

I shook my head. "No, I don't think I've got righteous anger. I've got the sort that makes God not happy with you. I don't know what to do. Mr Upson was right. He said it knots you up on the inside! I've got anger and unforgiveness and stuff but I just can't stop. St - one person in particular has really been a pain and Mum said I had to love her but I can't, I loathe her, she really hurt me and I want her to be hurt too and I'm annoyed and then there's my cou - someone else, and I'm scared about my mu - Mr Skinner! I told God and I thought he'd work everything out for my good but - oh dear - I've even been annoyed with God and not prayed!"

Mr Skinner sat down next to me.

"I said I'd try not to be angry. But I haven't. I mean, I haven't even tried really. I can't. I can't let it go. I know God wants me to forgive and be good and loving and all that but I can't, but I want him to forgive me for all the horrid things I do that upset him, so I must!"

"Samantha, dear! Listen. When you came to know Jesus, tell me: what happened?"

"I believed he died on the cross to take the punishment for all my horrid things so I could be friends with God."

"Exactly. Samantha, Jesus took the punishment for all your anger and hatred and unforgiveness. But after we come to Jesus, we still do things and say things and think things that hurt God. We've got to learn to confess our sin and the things that we do wrong every day. We must ask God to forgive us, and to help us to forgive others!"

"But Mr Skinner!" I said, frantically, "I can't do it!"

"Samantha, none of us can do it in our own power!" Mr Skinner leaned forward, earnestly. "When we read the Bible, we can see what God wants us to do and how he wants us to behave. It's hard - forgiving our enemies and things like that! But we must remember, we simply cannot live this new life by our own efforts. God doesn't expect us to! Jesus promises to give us the power to do whatever he asks us to do - the power of his Holy Spirit living in us. If he asks us to love someone, you can be sure he'll give us the power to love them! It's not something we can try desperately to do - you can't just conjure up love when you hate someone! We have to just be willing to let God do it in us - to change us, to love even our enemies through us. That's the key, I think, to your problem, Samantha! Are you willing to let God change your heart? To love others through you? Even the one who has hurt you so much?"

I nodded, miserably. "I think I must. Mustn't I?"

Mr Skinner shut his eyes, so I shut mine, and his calm voice was soothing.

"Lord, thank you for sending us your Holy Spirit who comes into our lives to make us like you, and who gives us the power to live to please you. Help us to listen and obey. Thank you Lord that you will give us the power we need to be obedient to you. Lord, thank you that you give us real power as you live your life in us. Power to overcome all the negative things that would drag us down and away from you. Samantha! Would you like to pray?"

"I'm sorry, Jesus," I whispered. "I've been cross with all those people. Especially that one person. More than cross. Furious. Lord, will you really give me the power to forgive? I want you to forgive me so much. Please help me. 'Cos I can't do it. I can't even try." Something flipped into my mind and I shuddered. Had Stacy really meant to hurt me? Maybe. Maybe not. But without a doubt, I had really meant to hurt her when I'd been so callous in the loos, and then later on when I hadn't let her sit with us and comforted her when she was so unhappy. In fact, I'd delighted in her misery. However much Stacy had got under my skin, I was certainly not blameless. She was naturally irritating, but I was just plain horrible. And I'd been horrible to Kendra and Alex too.

Slowly, and quietly, so Mr Skinner could barely have heard, I told God how awful I'd been. He knew of course, he just wanted me to tell him, to admit to it. I apologised for having made the Holy Spirit sad and asked God's forgiveness.

Gradually - just like the sun appearing on a cloudy day - I felt the Lord's warm presence again, only more vibrant and joyful than before. My eyes snapped open. Mr Skinner was smiling at me. I wondered in that moment if it wasn't so much what happened to you in life as how you reacted to it that mattered. After all, I'd chosen to be rotten to Stacy and the rest; I'd stopped reading my Bible and praying, hadn't I, the choice had been mine, not Stacy's or anyone else's!

"Mr Skinner, will God really work everything out for my good?"

"He says so, so trust him! But sometimes what God sees as good isn't what we see as good! At least, not at the time! Now, Samantha! If God asks you to do something, you must trust him to give you the power to do it, and obey what he tells you to do. OK?"

"Do something? Like what?" Actually, I didn't need to ask. At that moment, I knew. "Oh!"

Before anything else, God wanted me to go and see Stacy Morgan!

"But why! Why go and see her? What do you want me to say to her, God?" It was then that I had an uncomfortable feeling in my heart. "What! Apologise! Can't I just trust you to give me the power to forgive quietly in my heart, and ignore her?" Then I remembered how awful I'd been to her. I knew a trip to Stacy's house was inevitable if I wanted to keep in the beautiful warm presence of Jesus. "OK, I'll go. I don't want to grieve you again. I'll obey you! But I hope it's true what Mr Skinner says - that you'll give me the power, because this is the hardest thing I've ever had to do in my life!"

A Different View

I can't say I was filled with love for Stacy from the minute Mr Skinner prayed for me. I wasn't. But it was as if I had an assurance that Jesus was going to visit Stacy with me; I supposed that was something to do with the power of the Holy Spirit that Mr Skinner had been talking about. At any rate, although I wasn't overjoyed about going, I didn't feel as gloomy as I thought I would.

I'd never been to Stacy's house before, but I knew she lived in a road called Friar's Field on the new Rosemary Hedge estate, which had recently been built on what had been green fields on the edge of town, about ten minutes from my house. So that Sunday afternoon, I trudged along slushy paths to the new estate and wondered whether Rosemary Hedge was a person or a garden feature.

I asked a kid where Friar's Field was and he said it was at the bottom of the hill and turn left. As I started down the hill, I had a breathtaking view of Millstead, looking as if it had been sprinkled with icing sugar. Kids yelled as they slipped down the pavement near me and snowy roofed cars moved carefully along the gritted road. Snow was drip, drip dripping off the small uniformly red brick houses. My stomach turned a bit at the thought of seeing Stacy.

"What am I going to say to her, Jesus? I suppose I'll just have to trust you to give me the right words. Then maybe I can rush off home."

I stood on the corner of Friar's Field, which was a cul-de-sac, and put some gum in my mouth. I didn't know the number of Stacy's house. I asked a woman who was scraping snow off her car if she knew where the Morgan family lived and she said she didn't know any Morgans, and then I said they had a girl and a baby and then she pointed with a scraper to a small row of new terraced houses and said she thought it was number forty.

Number forty hadn't bothered to clear their path. They had a short front garden beyond a parking bay, with a low snowy fence and no gate. I took a deep breath and went up to the door.

"Jesus!" Yes, he was there. I could feel his presence, that calm and peace, that warm feeling in my heart. I was in his hands. A snowy Sunday afternoon! Would Mr and Mrs Morgan be in? I was curious about them. From what I recalled, from the few times I glimpsed them at church, they were nothing outstanding; her dad had glasses and her mum had a baby. I puzzled why Stacy had never asked me (or anyone else, so far as I knew) over to her house. I couldn't see that she'd be ashamed or anything of where she lived, it seemed quite nice.

It took ages for someone to answer the bell. In the end, I saw a shadowy figure through the glass panel, and her mum opened the door, dressed in a white towelling dressing gown, squinting at me as if she'd just woken up, even though it was half past two in the afternoon.

"Yes?"

"Er - hello, Mrs Morgan. Is Stacy in? I'm Sam."

Mrs Morgan blinked at me. For a minute I

thought maybe the reason Stacy didn't invite people home was because her mum was weird or something. I took a step backwards.

"Samantha Jones, from her school. I go to the church, I think I saw you there."

"Oh!" Her face broke into a smile. "Stacy's just gone to the shop for me. She'll only be about five minutes." I heard a baby wail, and Mrs Morgan said, "Oh, Ollie, Mummy's coming, darling! Samantha, do come in," and dashed inside. I pushed the door open wide, and tentatively stepped in, not sure whether I ought to go into somebody's house that I didn't really know. There was a pushchair in the tiny hall, and music from next door was thudding through the thin walls. Mrs Morgan appeared from a room on the right, carrying a plump baby. It was Stacy's little brother, Oliver. "Poor darling, it's his teeth. Shut the door, Samantha, it's cold today."

The baby had stopped crying and was staring at me as if I was the most interesting creature he'd ever seen in his life. I wasn't sure what you did with babies - I'd have been happier if Mrs Morgan was carrying a puppy, I really loved puppies - so I pulled a face and he giggled. Mrs Morgan laughed.

"You like Samantha, don't you, Ollie? You'll have to forgive me for not recognising you straight away, Samantha. Stacy's mentioned you - she bikes round to your house quite a bit, doesn't she, in Wingold Way? Well, it's nice to properly meet you. I've often said you could come here for tea, but she said you were busy. We never get to meet any of Stacy's friends!"

Stacy had never invited me for tea! I frowned as I followed Mrs Morgan into the little sitting room. It

115

had bare cream walls. There were toys strewn all over the floor. There wasn't much furniture - what there was looked shabby and the sofa wasn't new but then, neither was ours - and there didn't seem to be a hi-fi or VCR but then, maybe they were in a different room.

Mrs Morgan put the baby down. She indicated that I could sit on the sofa, and I did, narrowly missing plonking myself down on a squeaky toy. Mrs Morgan sat in a chair, right on the edge, coo-ing at Oliver. Then she asked if I had any baby brothers and sisters and I said "No!" as an image of my mum and Alex flashed into my mind; I shuddered at the thought of my mum sitting coo-ing over some infant sibling, dressed only in a dressing gown at half past two in the afternoon.

"Ollie's a late edition to the family, little sweetie! Our little miracle! I'm not religious, but I went to church a few times just to thank God for giving him to us after all these years. Best part of twelve years we've been trying for a little brother or sister for Stacy!"

The subject of all this trying gurgled happily as he tried to eat some of the carpet.

"Baby-waby-sweetie-darling-cutie! Harry - my husband - is thrilled to bits with him. Oh yes, you little cutie! Daddy's thrilled to have someone to play football with, isn't he, Ollie-wolly?"

"Girls play football," I pointed out, getting a bit embarrassed by this baby-talk.

"Ha ha! Mmm. Cutie! I wish Stacy would take more of an interest in him. But then, she was nearly thirteen when he was born. Big girl, isn't she, Ollie? And you're only a weeny mite, sweetie!"

"I'm sorry you missed the Gala yesterday," I said, trying to get Mrs Morgan off the baby-talk.

She didn't take her eyes off Oliver. "What Gala?"

I frowned. "At our school. It was 'The Christmas Heist' this year."

Mrs Morgan glanced at me, looking every bit as vacant as Stacy sometimes did. "Oh, that. Well, I couldn't come - not with Ollie. His teeth were giving him a very bad time. Sweetie cutie-pie! And Harry's having to work all hours - oh! Ollie! Did you bump yourself, darling? Do you want to come to mamma? No?"

"Stacy was a Christmas tree," I said.

Mrs Morgan chuckled. "Yes, she mentioned that. She loves her drama. She was in a lot of plays at her last school. Or was that the school before last? The last eighteen months are a bit of a blur; I had a difficult pregnancy, then Stacy and I had to live with her granny for a few months while Harry - never mind. Anyway," she added, rather dismissively, "She's a big girl now. She doesn't need her mummy and daddy fussing all over her like this little chappie does! Little lamb! And we don't trust baby-sitters, do we, Ollie, precious, when Ollie's poorly? No! Anyway," she glanced at me, cheerfully, "this Gala wasn't a big thing, was it?"

"It was to Stacy!" I said. And I couldn't help myself adding, "All the other parents were there!"

Before Mrs Morgan could reply - and she did look a bit taken-aback - there was a noise in what I presumed was the kitchen. Stacy came in. When she saw me, she almost dropped the packet of disposable nappies she was carrying.

I was a little disappointed that I still didn't feel any rush of God's love for Stacy. I stared at her, thinking about how irritating she was, and how she had my boy. Then I reminded myself that Jesus had wanted me to come and see her, so I quickly prayed for him to take over the situation, and forced myself to say hello. I could tell that she was uneasy having me in her home, which wasn't really surprising considering the last time we'd spoken I'd been absolutely repulsive to her. Her mum was gurgling all over the kid again in the most excruciating way. Was this why Stacy didn't invite people home? It wasn't something I'd want any of my friends to witness. The embarrassment of having your mum's brains turned to mush every time she clapped eyes on her baby, especially if you were trying to be cool!

"Want some juice or something?" said Stacy, shortly. I nodded. She wheeled round and silently led the way to the small kitchen. There, she shut the door, and turned to me. There was a defiant sparkle in her eyes. "Why are you here? Going to have another go at me?"

I was surprised. This was a fiery Stacy I hadn't seen before. The vacant, moony sort of expression was gone. She reminded me of one of the wild animals I'd seen in a recent TV documentary, trapped in its lair by someone with a camera and a large net. Could I at last be meeting the real Stacy Morgan? I prayed. I needed help. Then I heard myself say, "Stacy, look, I haven't come to argue or anything. I've just come to say I'm sorry for the rotten things I said. OK?"

Now it was her turn to look surprised. "Oh! Well, I was very upset you know. Especially when you said you'd never really liked me and stuff."

"Yes, I know, I've said I'm sorry." It was no use, I didn't like her. And she had Tim. But I was there for

Jesus. I'd done what he wanted, I'd apologised. There were no sweeping angel choirs and I didn't feel overflowing with love. But I could go home, now.

Then Mrs Morgan flapped into the kitchen squeaking that the little cutie had been sick. In the middle of all the flapping, Stacy caught my arm. "Come on, let's go upstairs to my room." Rather reluctantly, but wanting to escape having to help mop up the sick, I followed her.

Stacy's room was very pink and frilly. She had some stuffed toys on her bed. She also had a picture of my favourite band, 'The View', on her wall, and I said, "Cool!" when I saw it.

She shut the door behind her. Then I accidentally bumped into a bookshelf, and knocking a book to the floor, bent down to pick it up. It was called 'Tilly Goes To Stage School'. Stacy was apparently an avid Tilly fan; her shelf was crammed with the 'Tilly' school story books my mum had enthused about when I was eight saying they were charming little books for kiddies but that I'd never bothered to read because Tilly seemed such a drip. Something clicked in my brain. I wouldn't have been surprised to find those stories were full of the type of girls who said 'preposterous'.

"I used to read them when I was a kid," said Stacy, trying to sound casual.

"I'm sorry your parents didn't come to see the school play, Stacy."

Her face went bright red. I was horrified - she started to cry.

"Stacy, come on, things aren't that bad!" I found myself sitting next to her, with my arm placed round her shoulders. Then it all came out. Stacy blubbed and blurted her way through her life story. Apparently everything in her life had just been great until about a year and a half ago when her mum got pregnant. Stacy had been pushed aside in the excitement. Then her dad had lost his job, and Mr and Mrs Morgan had been panic stricken what with the new baby on the way and no money coming in, and Mrs Morgan had become ill. So Stacy and her mum had gone to live with her granny in London for a few months whilst her dad sorted out a new job - apparently not a very well paid job - in Millstead. Stacy had finished up going to three different schools in the past eighteen months.

"My mum was always interested in my drama and everything!" she finished off, wiping her eyes, "But when he came, everything was ruined."

'He', I realised, was Oliver. "Stacy! It's not your brother's fault. He's just a baby!"

"They just dote on him and no-one cares about me anymore. All they think about is money and the baby. Dad's at work all the time doing all the overtime he can. He's even working today. When he comes home he's just all over Oliver. And my mum - Sammy, you'd think Oliver was the baby Jesus! Sometimes I think I don't really matter at all!"

I was appalled, she sounded so bitter. Was she just being her usual over-dramatic self?

"I haven't got any friends! I had friends before we moved to granny's, friends I knew since I was two! But now, I'm a stranger and no-one likes me. Not even you, and I did want to be friends with you. I don't fit in anywhere, not even at home!"

I was going to say, no-one likes you? - you've got

Tim! But I didn't. Instead, I found myself saying, "Stacy, Jesus loves you. He really does. I know he does because he sent me round here today."

"Sammy!" A big tear rolled down her nose. "I was so desperate to have a friend, but I wasn't much of a friend to you! I knew you liked Tim. I could see you did. But I liked him too, and when he was nice to me, I couldn't help myself. He really likes me. Me!"

Oh! I took my arm away from her shoulders. Jesus! I thought. Help me! I'm going to murder her! But amazingly, the feelings of anger I expected to rise up in me didn't come. They just didn't. What did come instead was a feeling of real strength. I put my arm round her again.

"Sammy, I'm sorry. I don't know who or what I am. Sometimes I think I'm just a pretend person from a book, just a fantasy someone made up."

"No. I think there's a real Stacy underneath all the play-acting." I wasn't sure the real Stacy was a very nice Stacy. But she was infinitely more understandable than the false Stacy.

She grasped my hand. "Were you making it up that you didn't like me? Were you, Sammy? Did you like me all along, really?"

I couldn't lie. But neither could I say: "Well - no. I didn't!" So I just said, "Stacy, listen. You shouldn't have to play-act to make friends. It doesn't work. You should try being yourself. Drama and fantasy and escapism is all very well on stage. But not in real life."

"I'm not a real Christian, either. You're a Christian. But I'm not, really. Am I?"

"You could be. You could ask Jesus into your heart and he'd come in and give you a new clean life on the inside. You don't have to pretend with him. He knows exactly what you are on the inside, and he still loves you." Then I heard myself say, and I was astonished that I really meant it, "I'll pray for you anyway." I offered her some gum. "Better go, now."

On the way out, I saw Mrs Morgan, cuddling Oliver in the hall. "Samantha! Are you going?"

"Yes. Bye, Oliver! Goodbye, Mrs Morgan." I added as an afterthought, "Why don't you come to our church play next Sunday evening, Mrs Morgan? Stacy's great in it. She's the star."

I slung my hands in my pockets as I started to walk back home. Jesus had got me to go to Stacy's house for a reason, more than for just apologising; he'd shown me something about her, and yes, I would pray. I still didn't like her. But God loved her. And now I had more of an idea why she was so totally - Stacy.

I was still deep in thought when I got home. Alex was there, drinking coffee in the living room with my mum and Kendra, who were both laughing at some silly joke he was telling. It struck me that Kendra laughed a lot more than she used to. As soon as I walked in, she walked out into the kitchen, but it wasn't personal - her mobile phone had bleeped.

"Sam!" said my mum. "Alex was just talking about the dress rehearsal on Friday. You must have finished that Hawaii project by now. Why don't you go along, love, and help out?"

I thought of Stacy and Tim. I may have made my peace with Stacy, but could I face the thought of seeing them both together?

"No," I said, glumly, "don't think so."

"Oh, that's all right, producing plays isn't everyone's idea of fun!" Alex sounded light-hearted. "Samantha! David's been helping me on the organising side. He's really blossomed."

David! What had Tim said? David fancied me! I thought of lanky, wet David and winced. Alex was telling Mum about some of David's 'excellent ideas' now. It occurred to me that Alex didn't want me involved after all - why should he? I'd hardly made myself pleasant to him lately, had I? But what could I do about that? I wandered into the kitchen to get a coke. Kendra wasn't talking on the phone now. She was clutching it, staring out of the kitchen window. I remembered some of her nasty words to me - and some of my nasty words back. Ought I apologise to her, too? She turned to me, and tried to sound casual. "Well, that's that. You'll be relieved to know I'm going home. Tomorrow."

Wow! The best Christmas tidings I could ever hope for! But I didn't yell "Hooray! God is good!" Somehow, it just didn't seem appropriate, because something about Kendra didn't seem right. She wasn't pale. Even if she was, it would be a job to know under all that foundation and wads of blusher. But she looked strained, and hardly brimming over with joy at the prospect of going home.

"What's up?" I said, surprised, "I thought you'd be glad to leave us. We're boring old 'religious nuts', aren't we, in your opinion?" She shrugged and tried to look cool but it didn't quite work. I frowned. I didn't understand. I just thought she was being her usual moody, unfathomable self. It was only later, when I was walking past the open door to the spare room

123

and saw Kendra hugging my mum as they packed her suitcase together, that I wondered if Kendra had been jealous of me, of my close relationship with Mum, something she had't got with Aunty Ann. The more I thought about that, the more sense it made.

It looked as if Mr Upson had been right: both Kendra and Stacy were deeply unhappy. It just took a different view, God's view, for me to really see it.

Friends

There were about fifty people in the church hall. A small amount compared with the colossal crowd that turned out for 'The Christmas Heist' at the school, it was true, but I had a feeling that everyone who was meant to come that evening was there.

Alex's theory that people who wouldn't usually come to church would make the effort - even in the snow! - to see their children in a nativity play had been right. There were people in the hall I didn't recognise, as well as many that I did. Relatives and friends of the kids who were even now trilling 'Away in a Manger' so appealingly - apart from the boy who'd wanted to be a sheepdog and wouldn't stop barking - had their eyes glued to the stage, which was full of nativity characters.

I was standing, because there weren't any spare chairs. Mum and Mrs Kettle were sitting in the back row. I could hear our neighbour clucking fondly about the costumes, which some of the kids' mothers had made out of the usual tinsel, tea towels, aged sheets and cardboard. Old Edna and her friend - who'd said earlier she wasn't stopping - were sitting by Mr Upson and Maurice Watt. I was surprised to see Mr Watt clapping almost as madly as the doting parents at the end of the carol.

Then the lights flashed on and off and someone said, "Oh no, a power cut!", but it was only David being technical as Stacy came on in her guise as the time traveller. Of course, the audience weren't expecting that. With Stacy's appearance, the whole show took off. She threw her heart and soul into the part. I suppose most people who knew her thought that was because she was just a good actress, but I wondered if she had an extra incentive that night to act well. When I'd arrived that evening, she'd grabbed me, her eyes dancing with an excitement that nearly made her look passably pretty as she nodded towards her parents who were sitting in the front row with little Oliver.

"Thanks for inviting them, Sammy!"

I was going to say "I didn't!" but then I remembered I had. Well, I'd invited her mum. But I thought the presence of the Morgan family wasn't to do with the invitation. Maybe Mrs Morgan had felt badly after all at missing her daughter's performance as a Christmas tree in front of the school and all those other parents.

The production moved on, and everything went dark except for a single spotlight on Dinah, dressed as Mary in flowing blue robes (I don't know where she got them). She stood there, gently weeping, because they'd killed her Son Jesus.

Mum said afterwards that this was the single most moving performance in the play. I thought she was right. There was complete silence in the hall. Then Stacy appeared again, acting with believable shock as she apparently realised that the baby she'd just seen was the man who'd been crucified.

Then it was scene three, and Tim was there, holding a mobile phone and pretending to use his dad's laptop computer to indicate that it was the present day. He tried his best in the part, but he looked very self conscious and frankly, Stacy made him look even worse than he was just because she was so accomplished. But a strange thing happened: when he 'preached the gospel', everyone listened. And Mum said later that Tim was scattering the seed of the good news about Jesus, and in some hearts, it would germinate.

I thought the whole building would fall down, so thunderous was the applause at the end! The cast - and David, and Alex - all piled on the stage and everyone took a bow. I was pleased for them, of course. But I really did feel left out.

"It's Stacy's fault!" I said to myself, "I should've been - " I shook my head. "No, I had the choice. I could've been involved. Jesus! I chose not to, for whatever reason. It isn't her fault. Not really. Even if it is, or was, I forgive her. Yes, I do, with your help, Lord." And I clapped with the rest.

Mr Skinner clambered on the stage and announced that next week at the church there'd be a carol service which he would love everyone to go to, and a short service on Christmas day, too. Then he said there were refreshments, and there was a mad dash for the long trestle tables at the back of the hall which were filled with cakes and good things.

I ate a couple of scones, and then decided to go and congratulate the actors. I pushed past lots of excited little kids dressed as angels and wise men and shepherds who were running round the hall, reluctant to take their costumes off. They kept coming up to me and shouting, "Sammy! Did you see me? Sammy! I was an angel! Sammy! Sammy!"

I eventually found my way to the room behind the stage. Alex, Mr Skinner, David, Dinah and Stacy were in there toasting their success in Coke and orange juice.

"Wonderful!" said Mr Skinner, "Truly wonderful!"

"I saw Maurice Watt clapping," said Dinah, "he's the one that shouted 'bravo' and whistled."

"Rubbish!" said her brother, "He hasn't got the teeth for it."

"It was Mr Upson then," Dinah replied.

"He's got even less teeth."

"Hello, Sammy!" said David, suddenly, "Er - didn't see you standing there."

Quietness fell on the little group. All eyes were fixed on me.

Tim smiled. "We really missed you being involved, Sam."

I didn't say, "I'll bet!", although I felt like it.

"They were brilliant, weren't they, Sam!" said Alex.

"Yes, they were. That's what I came to say. Well done, everyone. It was great."

"Was I great, Sam?" asked Tim, "I mean, what did you think?"

What an opportunity, I thought, to completely trash his wooden performance, make him feel as small as I'd felt when he chose Stacy instead of me! I sighed. God didn't want me to be unkind to him, and I wanted to please God, not make him sad again. Anyway, God saw the heart, didn't he? Maybe something in Stacy's heart really appealed to Tim. But what about me? I was beginning to doubt I'd ever find a nice boy of my own.

Tim was waiting for me to say something, but in all truthfulness I couldn't say he was a great actor. He wasn't. So I told him, "One or two people said when you spoke about Jesus there was a 'powerful silence'."

Then Stacy said, "And me, Sammy?"

Oh! Another opportunity - but no. "Stacy, you know you were good. So was Dinah."

"Dinah," announced Stacy, theatrically, "was sublime!"

"Eh? I thought she was good," said Tim.

"Sublime means good," grinned Alex, "awesome! I thought you were meant to be brainy?"

The others sniggered, and Tim rolled his eyes in a comical way. Then Dinah said, with a sigh, "I dunno. We practised for weeks, and it was over so quickly. What're we going to do with ourselves now we haven't got rehearsals to go to?"

"Enjoy Christmas," suggested Alex.

They started to dissect the performance amongst themselves, and I noticed Tim put his arm loosely round the shoulders of the exuberant Stacy. She was being all actressy and false, and quite repellant. I preferred the Stacy I'd met in her bedroom - the contrite Stacy with faults and problems, but nevertheless real. At least I presumed that was the real Stacy, and not just another act.

I decided to sneak off. It was daft to feel depressed, but they'd all pulled together to achieve something for Jesus, hadn't they, and I wasn't part of it. Still, I thought, ruefully, I'd spent so much time on that Hawaiian project I'd come top in geography and the teacher had commended me for a very thorough piece of work and said he'd been particularly impressed by the meticulous detail regarding the canning of pineapples which must have taken me hours. And hours. And hours.

I didn't want to go and sit with my mum. She was chatting animatedly with Mr and Mrs Morgan. Mrs Morgan had almost dropped poor Oliver, she'd been clapping so hard at the end. And I had a feeling it was Mr Morgan who'd done the whistling. I just hoped my mum wasn't going to get broody; she was smiling adoringly at the baby. I thought of her excitement when Alex had brought us a real Christmas tree yesterday - the first real one we'd ever had. We normally just used the tatty tinsel one we stuffed in the cupboard every year. As people and children buzzed around me, I had the curious impression of being in the middle of a crowd and yet solitary. The sensation reminded me of what Stacy had once said about being alone in the universe.

"Sammy!" called old Edna, "Someone's opened the doors. Can you shut 'em?"

"OK." I nodded, and stood there for a moment, my head stuck round the doors, watching the snow falling gently on the pavement outside. I took a deep breath and - oh, wonderful. I felt the calm presence of Jesus there with me. I wasn't alone. I never ever would be.

"Sammy!" Dinah tapped me on the shoulder. "What're you doing?"

"Eh? Oh, I'm just watching the snow."

"I really am sorry you didn't keep coming to rehearsals."

"Ah, well!"

She looked truly concerned and lowered her

voice. "Are you upset about my brother? Is that what's been wrong? D'you like him, and don't want to see him with Stacy? I won't tell anyone."

I flushed scarlet. "No! Of course not." Then I felt bad about lying. "Dinah, I did like Tim. I mean, I do. But it's all right. I'm fine."

"Oh. OK. You know, I heard him talking to David about this girl called Iona who goes to Parkside. I hope he doesn't dump Stacy before Christmas. That would be awful for her, wouldn't it?"

"Oh!"

"He's always fancying different girls."

"Really?" Maybe I'd had a narrow escape from heartbreak, then! I'd thought Tim was a really nice boy, and maybe he was, but if he was always switching his affections to different girls, well, I didn't much like the sound of that. I had a sudden thought. Perhaps God had protected me from going out with Tim! I didn't know. I realised I didn't feel thrilled, or even any sneaking hope, that Tim would dump Stacy - and certainly not before Christmas! She'd be devastated. I found some chewing gum in my pocket. Poor Stacy! I bit my lip. Without a doubt, there was - what? - compassion in my heart for her. God had put it there!

"I think Stacy's going to need her friends if my brother does finish with her!" said Dinah, "Don't you?"

"Yes, Dinah. I do."

"What happened to your cousin? She's not here, is she? The girl who looks like a model?"

"Kendra? She's gone home." I called to mind the scene of a week ago. Yes, Kendra had gone. Aunty Ann and Bo had sorted out their 'life journies' and

131

were going home in a haze of 'cosmic peace' - quite quickly, as it happened, because the Department of Social Security wanted to see Bo about his benefit. Although I couldn't pretend to be upset that my cousin had gone home, I marvelled at how God was at work in her life - because he was, through a growing loving relationship with my mum. She'd even asked Aunty Ann if she could come back to see the play, which struck me as astounding, because she hadn't shown the slightest bit of interest in it, but Bo had said no. So there'd been a tearful farewell. She even looked sorry to say goodbye to me.

"God works in mysterious ways," Mum had said. And, of course, she was right.

"What's this! Some sort of meeting?" Alex was there now.

"Just looking at the snow," said Dinah.

"Let's hope it's warmer in a few weeks, Dinah, for your baptism!"

"Dinah!" I exclaimed. "Are you getting baptised?"

"Yes, Jesus was baptised so I want to be. Besides, I love him so much, I want to do what he says."

I stared. I'd never thought of being baptised before. Mum had been baptised when she was sixteen, and I sort of thought you had to wait till then at least. Dinah was just twelve. But she really wanted to do it and knew exactly why; not only did she want to do it because Jesus had done it, and it said we should do it in the Bible, but she also said she really understood what it meant. I never had before, but as she started to explain it, I began to see more clearly.

"Just as Jesus died and was resurrected to a new

life, so we are too, when we believe in him. Believing in Jesus is just like getting a new life. Jesus says that we should be baptised. I've never been baptised. I want to obey Jesus. I just feel it's the next step for me to take. "

I was very impressed by that. But the thought of getting a public bath in front of loads of people made me shiver. Did I want people to see me looking like a drowned rat? But perhaps it was something I'd have to think (and pray) about.

Dinah went back into the church then, and I was about to go, too, but Alex stopped me.

"I've got a confession to make."

"Oh?" What was he going to tell me? That he and Mum were getting married? That he had six kids that he wanted me to meet in the hope we might one day become a big happy family? Mum wanted a baby? What?

"I've never been baptised. I'm scared of water. Crazy, isn't it? I'm a bit embarrassed about it. So keep it to yourself."

"Well, I haven't been baptised either."

"Maybe we'll get baptised together one day!" He smiled. "Sammy, you don't mind me being friends with your mum very much, do you? I mean, you and me, we're friends too, aren't we?"

"Come on!" Mr Skinner bustled past, with Mr Upson and a couple of other oldies, muttering something about wanting to give them a lift home before we all got snowed into the church hall.

"Love, joy, peace, patience, kindness, goodness, faithfulness, gentleness and self control," Mr Upson was saying, "All the fruit of the Spirit in our lives! God is good. Isn't God good, Mr Skinner?"

"Yes, he is good, now pray the car starts," said Mr Skinner, ushering him out. I resolved to write out Christmas cards for both of them that night. Maybe I ought to put 'thanks' in both cards and 'sorry for letting you down about the play' in Mr Skinner's. I hadn't bought a card for Kendra or Stacy, either. I thanked God silently for giving me insight into both their lives. I remembered how I couldn't live this new life, the life of pleasing God, becoming more and more like Jesus, in my own power. Perhaps I ought to do something to show God I was serious about following him... I should certainly start by trying to love him more, be with him more, obey him more... and I knew that Jesus was going to be there with me, helping me all the way.

It struck me then that I hadn't written out a card for Alex - I hadn't even bought him a gift. He was stood there, looking a little nervous, waiting for an answer to his question - "We're friends, aren't we?"

I thought of that bit in the Bible which says, 'And we know that in all things God works for the good of those who love him, who have been called according to his purpose...' What had Mr Skinner said in the church: sometimes what God sees as good isn't what we see as good? I knew I had to trust him; after all, he knew more about what was the best thing for me than I did.

I nodded. "Yes Alex," I said, firmly, "we're friends."

A LITTLE BIT EXTRA

Facing Pressure

Pressure, pressure, pressure. Life can be full of stress. Exams, family strife, the future. Sometimes things get so difficult we just don't know how to handle it. Sam faces pressure in this book. She felt pressure from friends and family. We have to realise that sometimes we can't please everybody. It is more important to know if we are pleasing God or not. Ask yourself – What would Jesus do?

Bitterness and strife

Have you ever met someone who has totally changed your life? From the time Jesus enters our life things become radically different. Jesus said that we should do to others as we would have them do to us. This is a hard thing to do without His help and power in our lives. When Jesus and His Word is alive in our hearts we find that his love is stronger. We can even love people that we find it hard to love when Jesus is in control.

Dealing with hurts

At times things happen in our lives which are upsetting and hard to handle. It's then that we need God's help more than ever. Sometimes we can be so upset that we stop praying. Reacting in this way harms us even more. Speak to another Christian friend who you trust. Share your problems with God. He is always available. He knows what it is like to feel hurt and he loves you – remember that!

Wrong Attitudes
Do you ever bottle up your anger, hatred and annoyance. Feelings like that have to be dealt with or they will make everything worse. Bad attitudes come from the sin in our hearts. Ask Jesus to take control of your heart, emotions and life. Jesus died on the cross to save us from the sin that can destroy our lives and make us bitter and twisted inside. Jesus' presence in our lives is like having a brand new life. He completely changes us from the inside out and makes us a new creation.

Hurting people hurt others
It's so easy to hurt other people, sometimes without meaning to. You know what it's like to feel hurt and rejected yourself. Remember that when people do and say things that hurt and upset you there is always a reason for it. Perhaps they are jealous of you or they have problems of their own. When people are hurting they can take it out on other people - even their best friends. We need to see other people as God sees them. God tells us that we should show love and mercy to other people. The Bible tells us that we should pray for those who despitefully use us.

Decision making
"Should I or shouldn't I?" Sometimes we are faced with quite difficult decisions. Sometimes we want to do something but we have a sneaking suspicion that it wouldn't be right. Sam wanted to go to the Halloween Party but in the end decided that it wouldn't be right. We should always ask God to help us make decisions like this. Remember that God promises to be with us at all times and he has promised to instruct us and guide us. Psalm 32:8

Ten Boys who changed the World

by Irene Howat

Billy Graham, Brother Andrew, John Newton, George Muller, Nicky Cruz, William Carey, David Livingstone, Adoniram Judson, Eric Liddell, Luis Palau.

Would you like to change your world? These ten boys grew up to do just that! Find out how Eric won the race and honoured God; David became an explorer and explained the Bible; Adoniram was in prison and praised God; Nicky joined the gangs and then the church; Luis was changed by God and God changed others; William translated the Bible and gave God's word to India; George rescued orphans and was trusted with millions; Andrew smuggled Bibles into Russia and brought hope to thousands; John captured slaves but God used him to set them free; Billy preached and God used him to change people all around the world. Read this book and find out what God wants you to do!

ISBN: 1-85792-579-3

Ten Girls who changed the World

by Irene Howat

Corrie ten Boom, Mary Slessor, Helen Keller, Joni Eareckson Tada, Jackie Pullinger, Isobel Kuhn, Amy Carmichael, Evelyn Brand, Gladys Aylward, Catherine Booth.

Would you like to change your world? These ten girls grew up to do just that! Find out how Corrie saved lives and loved Jesus during World War II; Mary saved babies in Africa and fought sin; Gladys rescued 100 Chinese children and trusted God; Joni survived a crippling accident and still thanked Jesus; Amy rescued orphans and never gave up; Isobel taught the Lisu about Christ and followed him; Evelyn obeyed God in India and taught others to as well; Jackie showed love in awful conditions in Hong Kong; Helen showed determination and discovered God and Catherine rolled up her sleeves and helped the homeless! Read this book and find out what God wants you to do!

ISBN: 1-85792-649-8

You've read 'This New Life'
but what about the first
book in this series?

Sheila Jacobs

A Different Life

Meet Sammy. Sammy wants a different life. What she really wants is to grow up fast like her friends have - but how does she do it without her mum finding out?

Then Luce moves in next-door and Sammy falls for him. He'd be the perfect boyfriend and the girls would be so impressed - how can she get his attention?

But as Sammy discovers more about Luce and the girls at school she starts to wonder if this is really the 'different life' she's been looking for. Why is growing up so difficult?

Then Sammy finds out that there is someone who can give her a new and changed life - but what will her friends think?

ISBN: 1-85792-590-4

Sheila Jacobs

Aliens and Strangers

In this book we meet Jane for the very first time. She hates her school and doesn't have many friends. The only thing she enjoys is writing science fiction.

But are Jane's stories just fiction? Or have aliens really landed on earth?

Is their mission to break up families - will Jane's family be next?

Jane discovers there is only one person she can turn to, but will he help her?

ISBN: 1-85792-279-4

Sheila Jacobs

Rollercoaster Time

Jane is desperate to know the future. She is sick fed up of all the ups and downs in her life and she is worried about what lies ahead. Should she try and find out?

Someone at school shows Jane a magazine called Future Fantastic that promises to show you the future and what's to come! Astrology! Tarot Cards! Palmistry! Your love life written in the stars.

Will Jane be fooled or will she trust the one person who really knows what is round the corner?

ISBN: 1-85792-385-5

Sheila Jacobs

Something to Shout About

Jane is back in her old home town of Gipley but things are not the same as they were, in more ways than one.

Heather's mum has got a slimy new boyfriend, Heron introduces everybody to her very good-looking brother, Woody, and it seems as though Heather's church is now going to get closed down. Woody persuades Jane and Heather to spear head a 'Save our Church' campaign.

Soon the girls are up to their necks in banners, slogans and campaign strategies. However nobody has thought to ask God what he thinks of the whole situation. Eventually Jane learns a valuable lesson about prayer and seeking God's will in every situation.

ISBN: 1-85792-488-6

CHRISTIAN FOCUS

Good books with the real message of hope!

Christian Focus Publications publishes biblically-accurate books for adults and children.

If you are looking for quality bible teaching for children then we have a wide and excellent range of bible story books - from board books to teenage fiction, we have it covered.

You can also try our new Bible teaching Syllabus for 3-9 year olds and teaching materials for pre-school children.

These children's books are bright, fun and full of biblical truth, an ideal way to help children discover Jesus Christ for themselves. Our aim is to help children find out about God and get them enthusiastic about reading the Bible, now and later in their life.

Find us at our web page:
www.christianfocus.com